He'd hoped that she would remember the two of the

"Do you recall where asked. "From Chri February?"

Her head jerked up. She said nothing as her surprised gaze locked with his, but her face paled and she dropped the glass in her hand. It hit the hardwood floor, shattering like a gunshot, ice shooting out, the last of the cola puddling at her feet. But she didn't move. She stared at him as if seeing a ghost. No doubt a ghost of Christmas Past.

"*You?*" she cried, all the ramifications coming at Mach-two speed.

"*The baby—*"

"*It's ours...?*"

Dear Harlequin Intrigue Reader,

Need some great stocking stuffers this holiday season for yourself and your family and friends? Harlequin Intrigue has four dynamite suggestions—starting with three exciting conclusions.

This month, veteran romantic suspense author Rebecca York wraps up her special 43 LIGHT STREET trilogy MINE TO KEEP with *Lassiter's Law*, and Susan Kearney finishes her action-packed HIDE AND SEEK miniseries with *Lovers in Hiding*. Julie Miller, too, closes out the MONTANA CONFIDENTIAL quartet with her book *Secret Agent Heiress*. You won't want to miss any of these thrilling titles.

For some Christmastime entertainment, B.J. Daniels takes you west on a trip into madness and mayhem with a beautiful amnesiac and a secret father in her book *A Woman with a Mystery*.

So make your list and check out Harlequin Intrigue for the best gift around...happily ever after.

Happy holidays from all of us at Harlequin Intrigue.

Sincerely,

Denise O'Sullivan
Associate Senior Editor
Harlequin Intrigue

A WOMAN WITH A MYSTERY

B.J. DANIELS

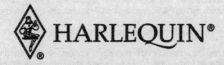

HARLEQUIN®

TORONTO • NEW YORK • LONDON
AMSTERDAM • PARIS • SYDNEY • HAMBURG
STOCKHOLM • ATHENS • TOKYO • MILAN • MADRID
PRAGUE • WARSAW • BUDAPEST • AUCKLAND

ISBN 0-373-22643-8

A WOMAN WITH A MYSTERY

This edition published by arrangement with Harlequin Books S.A.

® and TM are trademarks of the publisher. Trademarks indicated with ® are registered in the United States Patent and Trademark Office, the Canadian Trade Marks Office and in other countries.

Visit us at www.eHarlequin.com

Printed in U.S.A.

ABOUT THE AUTHOR

Born in Houston, B.J. Daniels is a former Southern girl who grew up on the smell of gulf sea air and Southern cooking. But like her characters, her home is now in Montana, not far from Big Sky, where she snowboards in the winters and boats in the summers with her husband and daughters. She does miss gumbo and Texas barbecue, though! Her first Harlequin Intrigue novel was nominated for the *Romantic Times Magazine* Reviewer's Choice Award for best first book and best Harlequin Intrigue. She is a member of Romance Writers of America, Heart of Montana and Bozeman Writers group. B.J. loves to hear from readers. Write to her at: P.O. Box 183, Bozeman, MT 59771.

Books by B.J. Daniels

HARLEQUIN INTRIGUE
312—ODD MAN OUT
353—OUTLAWED!
417—HOTSHOT P.I.
446—UNDERCOVER CHRISTMAS
493—A FATHER FOR HER BABY
533—STOLEN MOMENTS
555—LOVE AT FIRST SIGHT
566—INTIMATE SECRETS
585—THE AGENT'S SECRET CHILD
604—MYSTERY BRIDE
617—SECRET BODYGUARD
643—A WOMAN WITH A MYSTERY

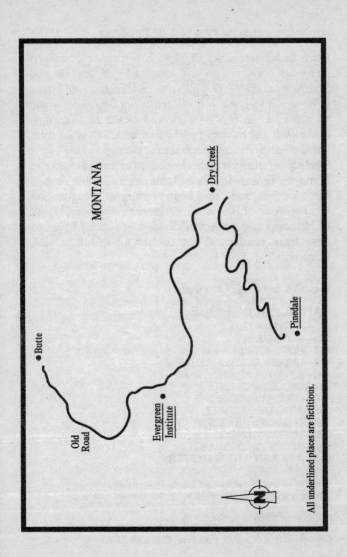

MONTANA

Butte

Old Road

Evergreen Institute

Dry Creek

Pinedale

N

All underlined places are fictitious.

CAST OF CHARACTERS

Holly Barrows—Someone had taken control of her mind—and her memory. Now they had her baby. But had they "sent" her to Private Investigator Slade Rawlins? Or was she starting to remember her past?

Slade Rawlins—The private investigator had his own reasons for wanting Holly to remember—*everything*.

Shelley Rawlins—Slade's twin knew more about their mother's murder than she thought—enough to get her killed.

Dr. Allan Wellington—The doctor might be dead, but he was far from forgotten.

Inez Wellington—How far would she go to keep her brother's legacy alive?

Police Chief L. T. Curtis and Norma Curtis—The cop and his wife were like family to Slade and his sister Shelley.

Dr. Fred Delaney—He'd been the Rawlins family doctor for years, but could he be trusted?

Carolyn Gray—The nurse was the only witness, and now she was missing.

Marcella Rawlins—Her murder had gone unsolved for twenty years—until her son stumbled across a letter.

Lorraine Vogel—The nurse knew where all the bodies were buried.

Jerry Dunn—The pharmacist was only doing what his father before him had done.

Acknowledgments:

Thanks to Randy Harrington, RPh, for his advice on hypnotic drugs; Marcia Proctor, CHt, RBT, for her technical input on hypnosis; Carmen R. Lassiter for her computer expertise and moral support; and as always the Bozeman Writers Group for keeping me honest.

Dedication:

With love and gratitude, this book is dedicated to Bill and Dorothy Heinlein. You are the in-laws I always dreamed of. Thank you for taking me into your wonderful family, for making me feel so welcome and for raising such a great son.

Prologue

Halloween

The pain. It dragged her up from the feverish blackness, doubling her over in a scream of anguish. Her eyelids fluttered, a flickering screen of light and dark. Three shadows moved at the end of the bed, silhouetted against a shaft of blinding light. They wavered in a whisper of dark clothing and low voices, hovering at her feet, waiting.

"Help me," she tried to say, but her mouth was cotton, her words lost in their whispers.

The shadows moved, blocking the blinding light. She blinked, focused. A scream tore from her throat as she saw them, really saw them. Her eyes locked open, her heart clamoring in her chest at the sight of their grotesque faces as they huddled around her. The three made no move to stop her from screaming and she knew from some place deep inside her that she couldn't be heard outside this room or they would have.

She tried to get up. Another pain shot through her. She pushed herself up on her elbows, suddenly lightheaded and sick to her stomach. She could feel the

agony again, coming like a speeding train toward her.
She had to get away before it was too late.

One of them stepped from the bright light, face hidden behind a hideous mask, voice muffled. "It will be over soon."

Her eyes widened, blood thundered in her ears. She knew that voice! Oh, my God!

Hands held her down as the pain accelerated, the macabre shadows a frenzied flicker of movement and whispers, the horrible whispers, suddenly rising in alarm.

She tried to see what was wrong, but her view was blocked, the hands strong holding her down. She squeezed her eyes shut against the horrifying images, against the paralyzing fear and the unimaginable pain. Gasping for each breath, she fought not to scream, fought not to lose her mind. But she knew it was already too late. The moment she'd seen their masked faces, she'd known. The moment she'd heard the familiar voice. The monsters had come to take her baby.

Chapter One

Christmas Eve

Aware only of the letter in his pocket, Slade Rawlins didn't feel the thick wet snowflakes spiraling down from the growing darkness or take notice of the straggling shoppers scurrying to their cars.

He strode down the street toward his office, oblivious to everything but the weight of the letter pressed against his heart, heavy as a stone.

"Ho! Ho! Ho!" A department-store Santa suddenly stepped from a doorway onto the sidewalk in front of him, a blur of red in the densely falling snow. "Merry Christmas!"

Startled, Slade jerked back in alarm as the Santa, his suit flocked with snow, thrust a collection pot at him with one hand and clanged his bell with the other.

Hurriedly digging in his pants pocket, Slade withdrew a handful of coins and dropped them into the pot, then sidestepped the man to get to his office door.

The stairs to the second floor were dimly lit, one of the bulbs out. But that was the least of his troubles. He took the steps two at a time, the sound of Christmas music, traffic and the incessant jangle of the Santa bell-ringer following him like one of Ebenezer Scrooge's ghosts.

"Bah humbug!" he muttered under his breath as he opened the door to Rawlins Investigations and, without turning on the light, went straight to the small fridge by the window. He pulled out a long-neck bottle of beer, unscrewed the cap and took a drink as he looked down on the small town from his little hole of darkness.

Outside, snowflakes floated down from a pewter sky, the cold frosting the edges of his window. Inside, the office was hotter than usual, the ancient radiator churning out musty-scented heat.

He could afford an office in the new complex at the edge of town. But he couldn't imagine himself there any more than he could imagine leaving this town. He felt rooted here, as if some powerful force held him.

And he knew exactly what that force was.

He shook off a chill in the hot room as the phone rang. He'd been expecting the call. "Rawlins."

"I heard you were down here a few minutes ago giving my people a hard time," snapped Police Chief L. T. Curtis.

Slade relaxed at the familiar rumble of the cop's voice. He'd heard it all his life. It had been as much a part of his childhood as the smell of his mother's bread baking. The thought gave him a twinge. Had nothing really been as it seemed?

"Did anyone tell you it's Christmas Eve?" Curtis asked sarcastically. "Why aren't you home decorating a damn tree or something?" Slade's father and Curtis had both been cops and best friends.

"I found new evidence in mom's case," Slade said, cutting to the chase. It was all he'd been able to think about since he'd discovered the letter. "I think I know who really killed her."

Curtis groaned. "Slade, how many times have we been down this road? I don't for the life of me understand why you keep pursuing this. The case is closed. It has been for twenty damned years. Her killer confessed."

"Roy Vogel didn't kill her," Slade said, rushing on before the chief could interrupt him. "I found a letter my mother wrote my aunt Ethel before she died."

"Aunt Ethel? The one who passed away in Townsend a couple weeks ago?" Curtis said. "I was sorry to hear about it."

Aunt Ethel had been a cantankerous spinster a good ten years older than Slade's mother. Because of some family disagreement years before the marriage, Ethel had never liked Slade's father, so had hardly ever come around.

"Yeah, well, she left everything to me, which amounted to several boxes of old letters," Slade said as he leaned against the radiator, needing the warmth right now. "Did you know my mother was seeing another man?" Even as he said the words, he had trouble believing them.

"Where the hell did you get an idea like that?"

"She as much as admits it in the letter."

"Bull," Curtis said. "Not your mother. She worshiped the ground your father walked on and you know it."

"I thought I did. But it seems my mother had a secret life none of us knew about."

"In a town like Dry Creek, Montana? Not a chance."

While relieved that Curtis was having trouble believing it too, Slade couldn't disregard what he'd found.

His mother's murder was one of the reasons he'd become a private investigator. He'd been the one who'd found her. Twelve years old, Slade had come home early from school and had to call his father at the police station to tell him. That day, he'd promised himself—and her—that he'd find her killer—no matter what his father said. Joe Rawlins had been afraid that Marcella's killer might come after his kids next and had told Slade to let him handle it.

Later that evening, the troubled young man who lived down the street was found hung in his garage. Roy Vogel had left a suicide note confessing to Marcella Rawlins's murder. All these years, Slade had never believed it. He'd always been suspicious of anything that wrapped up that neatly. But there had been no other leads. Until now.

"I just have a feeling about this," Slade said.

"Well, I'm telling you, you're all wrong, feeling or no feeling," Curtis said. "I wish to hell you'd just get on with your life and let your mother rest in peace."

"That's not going to happen until her murderer is brought to justice."

Curtis swore. "Damn, but you're a pain in the—"

"But you'll take a look at the letter tonight at Shelley's?" They'd all spent every Christmas Eve together as far back as Slade could remember. L. T. and Norma Curtis had been his parents' best friends and had finished raising Slade and his sister Shelley. But they'd been like family long before that.

"You haven't told Shelley?" Curtis asked.

"Nor do I intend to unless I have to."

"It will never come to that," the chief said. "Because you're dead wrong."

Slade hoped Curtis was right about that. But then there was the letter. The chief would know who had been friends with Marcella Rawlins twenty years ago. And if he didn't, his wife Norma would.

"Go Christmas shopping. Buy some eggnog. Give this a rest until after the holidays," Curtis advised, surely knowing his words were falling on deaf ears.

Once Slade got something in his head, nothing could stop him. "I'll see you tonight at Shelley's. I want you to see the letter. This can't wait until after the holidays."

"Merry damn Christmas then." Curtis hung up.

Slade replaced the receiver and turned again to the window. The snow fell in a silent white cloak, obliterating the buildings across the street. But he knew this town and everyone in it by heart.

Did that mean he'd known the man his mother had been seeing? Still knew him? He's still here, Slade thought. And he thinks he got away with murder. He doesn't know I'm coming for him. Yet.

He thought of what the chief had once told him about people trapped in their own lives, in their own illusions of reality, unable to get out, and wondered if he wasn't one of them. Well, then so was his mother's killer, he thought, as he raised his bottle, the snow falling so hard now he could barely see the Santa below his window, although he could still hear the bell.

It had been snowing the day he'd found his mother's body. He hadn't seen her at first—just the Christmas tree. It had fallen over on the floor. As he'd moved toward it, he was thinking the cat must have pulled it over. Then he saw her. Marcella Rawlins lay under a portion of the tree, a bright red scarf knotted tightly around her neck, one of the Christmas ornaments clutched in her hand. On the radio, Christmas music played and, as tonight, somewhere off in the distance, a seasonal Santa jangled his bell.

Behind him, the soft scuff of a heel on the hardwood floor jerked him from his thoughts. He remembered belatedly that he'd failed to shut and lock his office door. Damn.

"We're closed!" he called out, not bothering to turn around. He took another drink and watched the snow fall, waiting for the footsteps to retreat.

When they didn't, he turned, a curse on his lips.

She stood silhouetted against the dim light from the stairs, her body as sleek and curved as the long-neck in his hand and just as pleasing as the cold beer. She didn't move. Nor did she speak. And that was just fine with him.

He ran his hand down the neck of the sweating bottle, enjoying the slick wet feel of it as much as he liked looking at her. Something about her reminded him of another woman he'd known and with the lights off he could almost pretend—

The bell suddenly stopped, the snow silencing everything down on the street. Slade could hear the quickened beat of his heart, the radiator thumping out heat and the faint sound of Christmas music drifting from the apartment next door.

"Mr. Rawlins?" Her voice was as seductive as her silhouette and almost…familiar.

He frowned and tipped the bottle toward her in answer, telling himself he was letting his imagination run away with him.

"Do you mind if I turn on a light?" she asked.

He did. He was tired and all the holiday cheer and the letter had left him on edge. Why couldn't she just stand there? Or leave? He'd bet his pickup she wouldn't look half as good in the light. And once he'd seen her, he wouldn't be able to pretend anymore.

She flicked the light switch.

He blinked, too shocked to speak. He'd been wrong about the light. She looked even better than she had in silhouette. Dangerous curves ran the length of her, from the full, rounded breasts straining against the thin silk of her blouse beneath the open wool coat to the long, shapely legs that peeked between her skirt and her snowboots, all the way back up to her face. And, oh, what a face it was. Framed in a wild mane of curly dark hair. Lips lush. Baby-blues dark-lashed and wide.

It was a face and body he'd spent months trying to forget.

He swore under his breath, more in shock than anger, although he'd spent most of the last year looking for her, worrying that she was dead—and blaming himself for letting it happen.

"I need your help," she said, a slight catch in her voice. "I know it's Christmas Eve…"

He shook his head in disbelief. A thousand questions leapt into his mind, all having to do with where she'd been, what she was doing here now and why she'd left him. Oh yes, especially why she'd left him, he thought bitterly.

"What the hell do you think you—" He took a tentative step toward her, then stopped as he saw her expression. Blank as a wall. No recognition. She didn't know him!

He let out a colorful curse.

"I really shouldn't have bothered you." She turned to leave.

He knew if he had any sense at all, he'd just let her go. If only he'd done that the first time.

"Just a minute." He reached for her, afraid the moment he touched her, she would disappear again. Another one of Scrooge's ghosts.

His hand brushed hers. She turned back to him, her blue eyes glistening with tears. She didn't evaporate into thin air. Didn't disappear like a mirage before him. And after touching her, he knew she was most definitely flesh and blood. But not the woman he'd known.

This woman was a walking shell of that woman, and he couldn't help but wonder what had happened since to make her that way.

"I'm sorry, you just caught me by surprise," he said, looking into all that blue again. Just as he had a year ago, when she'd come running out of the snowstorm and into the street. He'd tried to stop his pickup in time, but the snow and ice— He'd jumped from his truck and run to her. She'd lain sprawled in the snow just inches from his bumper. When she'd opened her eyes in the headlights, they were that incredible blue—and blank. Not as blank as they were now. There'd been something in her expression…something that had hooked him from the moment his gaze had met hers.

"Here," he said, offering her a chair as he closed his office door, afraid she'd change her mind and leave. "What can I do for you?"

She seemed to hesitate, but accepted the chair he offered her, sitting on the edge of the seat, her handbag in her lap, her fingers clutching it nervously.

He leaned against the edge of his desk and stared down at her. Easy on the eyes, but hard on the heart, he thought. He knew better than to get involved with her again. But curse his curiosity, he had to know.

Last year when she'd come to in the street, he'd picked her up and put her in the cab of his pickup, planning to take her to the hospital. But she'd pleaded with him to just take her somewhere safe. She had no memory. No name. No past. But she'd been convinced someone was trying to kill her and had pleaded with him not to involve the police.

"I need your help," she said now.

"*My* help?" he asked, still looking for some recognition in her gaze. But it appeared she didn't know him from Adam! Either he wasn't that memorable or the woman had a tendency to forget a lot of things. "Why me?"

She shook her head and clutched her purse tighter. "I'm afraid this was a mistake." She started to get up.

He was on his feet, moving toward her. "No," he said a little more strongly than he'd meant to. "At least give me a chance."

She lowered herself back into the chair, but seemed apprehensive of him. Certainly not as trusting as last time, he thought with no small amount of resentment.

He'd taken her in and tried to unravel her past, believing she must be suffering from some sort of trauma.

But two months later, he was the one who'd gotten taken in. Just when he thought he might be making some progress into her past, she'd disappeared without a trace, along with a couple hundred dollars of his money and a half dozen of his case files. He'd spent months looking for her, fearing someone *had* killed her. Wanting to wring her neck himself.

And now she was back. Alive. And in trouble. Again.

"I'm afraid you're going to think I've lost my mind," she said, her voice as soft as her skin, something he wasn't apt ever to forget. She shivered as if her words were too close to the truth.

"Why would I think that?" he asked, wondering if she could just be playing him. It was too much of a coincidence that she'd come into his life twice—both times in trouble, on Christmas Eve and supposedly with no memory. At least, this time, no memory of him, it seemed.

"The help I need is rather unusual."

He pulled up a chair and sat down. "Try me."

She seemed to relax a little now that he wasn't towering over her, but she still clutched her handbag, still looked as if she might take off at a moment's notice. Is that what had happened last time? She'd gotten scared? Scared of what he was going to find out about her? Or had she just planned to rip him off the whole time? And all these months he'd been telling himself that she'd just gotten cold feet about what was happening between the two of them.

"I think someone stole my baby."

He stared at her. She had a child? "Wouldn't you *know* if someone had taken your child?"

"I know it sounds…crazy, but, you see, that's just it, I'm not sure."

Déjà vu. This would have been a good time to tell her he couldn't help her. Wasn't about to get involved in her life again. But he had to know who she was and where she'd been all this time. And why. Why she'd conned him. Why she'd stolen from him. Mostly, how much of it had been a lie.

"Why don't you start at the beginning," he suggested. "Like with your name."

"Oh, I'm sorry," she said with obvious embarrassment. She kneaded nervously at her purse and he could tell she was having more than second thoughts about coming here.

He gave her a smile. "Take your time."

Her answering smile was like bright sunlight on snow. Dazzling. And it had the same effect on him it had had a year ago.

"My name is Holly Barrows. I'm an artist. I live in Pinedale."

Pinedale? Just fifty miles over a mountain pass from here. Had she really been that close all these months? "How long have you lived there?" he had to ask.

"All my life."

So is that what had happened? Her memory had returned last year and she'd just gone home? It seemed a little too simple given that she'd been so convinced someone was trying to kill her. Not to mention that she'd stolen his money and case files—then apparently forgotten him. And Christmas past.

"Please go on," he encouraged.

"When I gave birth...." she said, the words seeming to come hard. "...I have little memory of the delivery. I think I was drugged."

"You gave birth in Pinedale?" he asked.

She shook her head. "I don't know where it was, just that it wasn't a normal hospital. I think the room was soundproofed and the doctors..." She looked away. Her hands trembled. "When I woke, I was in County Hospital. I was told that my baby was stillborn. I don't know how I got there. But I keep remembering hearing my baby cry. When I asked to see my baby at the hospital—" She stopped, seeming to be fighting to compose herself. "—I knew the infant they gave me wasn't mine."

He stared at her in shock. "The hospital let you see your stillborn baby?"

"See it, hold it, name it," she said in that same blank, distant voice. "So the mother knows it's really gone."

Sweet heaven. He couldn't imagine. "What made you think the baby wasn't yours if you never saw it right after the birth?"

She shook her head. "A mother knows her own baby."

He wondered if that was true. "What is it you think happened to *your* baby, presuming you're right and the baby was born alive at this other place?" Then replaced with a dead one? How plausible was that?

"I know how insane it sounds, but I keep having these flashes of memory. My baby was alive. Someone stole it."

Someone? The same someone she'd thought was trying to kill her a year ago?

She was wasting his time. It was obvious he wasn't going to get his money—or his case files—back. Nor any explanation, let alone satisfaction, for the heartache she'd caused him. She was a nutcase. A beautiful, desirable nutcase.

She fumbled to open her purse.

The movement should have concerned him. She might be going for a weapon. As crazy as she was, she might shoot him. But the way her hands shook, she wouldn't have been able to hit the broad side of a barn even if she pulled a howitzer from the bag.

She tugged out a tissue and wiped her eyes.

He'd heard enough, but still, he had to ask. "Why would someone want to take your baby?"

She glanced up, tears in her eyes. "I don't know. I just have this feeling that this isn't the first time they've done this. That there have been other babies they've stolen."

She was worse than he'd thought.

He rubbed a hand over his face, remembering something she'd said. "During the delivery, you mentioned the doctors. You saw them then?"

She shook her head, one glistening tear making a path down her perfectly rounded cheek. "Not their faces." She seemed to hesitate as if what she was about to say could be any worse than what she'd already told him. "They wore masks."

"Masks? You mean surgical masks?"

"Halloween masks with hideous monster faces." She avoided his gaze as she rooted around in her purse again. "I will pay you whatever you want to prove that I'm not crazy and to get my baby back."

He closed his eyes for a moment, taking a deep breath. And to think he used to fantasize about finding her. "When was 'his anyway?"

"Five weeks ago."

He nodded distractedly, wondering why it had taken her five weeks.

When he opened his eyes, she had the checkbook in her hand, her expression filled with hopefulness as she looked up at him again.

Sweet heaven. He couldn't believe that a part of him would gladly leap on his noble steed and ride off to battle evil for this damsel in distress yet again. Except that she'd punctured a hell of a hole in his armor the last time around. She'd gone straight for his heart, and he wasn't apt to forget it, no matter how desirable, how beautiful or how crazy and in need of help she was this time around.

"I'm sorry, but I'm afraid I can't help you," he said, getting to his feet.

Slowly, she lowered her gaze to her lap. He watched her put the checkbook back into her purse and rise from the chair.

"I'm sorry to have wasted your time," she said without looking at him.

He watched her walk to the door and thought he should at least suggest she seek medical help. Did she know a good psychiatrist?

But he let her go. She was either a crackpot, or a con artist. Her name probably wasn't even Holly Barrows.

He listened as her boot heels tapped down the stairs, and he waited for the sound of the door closing on the street below, before he picked up his beer bottle and went to the window again.

It had stopped snowing, the sky dark, the air cold against the glass. He watched her hurry to a newer SUV parked at the curb. Out of habit, he jotted down her license-plate number when her brake lights flashed on.

Why had she come to him with this latest ludicrous story? Hadn't she gotten what she'd come for the last time?

She pulled out into the street, and he had to fight the urge to run after her.

As he started to turn from the window, he caught a movement on the sidewalk below and looked down. The Santa bell-ringer no longer had his pot. Or his bell.

He was looking after the retreating Holly Barrows and talking hurriedly into a cell phone.

Slade felt a jolt as the Santa glanced up toward his office window. The look was brief, but enough. Slade swore and scrambled around his desk and out of the office. He launched himself down the stairs, nearly falling on the wet steps, his mind racing faster than his feet, and burst through the door to the sidewalk.

The Santa was gone—except for his red hat and white fake beard lying on the pavement.

The quiet snowy darkness settled over Slade as he stared down the now-empty street. He'd seen the Santa's alarmed expression when he'd looked up and spotted Slade at the window, recalled the agitated way the man had been talking into the cell phone.

Worry clutched at him the way Holly Barrows had clutched at her purse. Sweet heaven, could she have been telling the truth this time? More important, had she been telling the truth a year ago when she'd thought someone was trying to kill her?

Suddenly a thought lodged like a stake in his heart. If she wasn't crazy, if Holly Barrows really had been pregnant and had delivered a baby five weeks ago, then— If nothing else, he'd always been good at math.

He stumbled back against the side of the building as he stared down the street in the direction her car had disappeared. If there really had been a baby, there was a damned good chance it was his.

Chapter Two

"Are you all right?" Shelley asked him as she sliced a loaf of homemade cranberry bread. Her kitchen smelled the way their mother's used to. Something was always cooking.

"Fine, why?" He leaned against the counter to watch her, trying to put on his best holiday face.

It was obvious to anyone who saw them together, that Slade and Shelley were siblings. Shelley's hair was the same thick, dark blond as his, her eyes a little paler hazel. They'd both taken after their father's side of the family. Like him, she had the Rawlins' deep dimples. They were, in fact, fraternal twins.

"You think I can't tell when something is bothering you?" she asked. "Something *more* than Christmas."

Christmases were always hard on him. This one was especially tough after what he'd found in his mother's letter, but he wasn't going to tell her that.

"Remember that woman? The one I met last year about this time?"

She kept cutting the bread. "The one who couldn't remember who she was. You called her Janie Doe." She frowned. "I remember how worried you were about her when she disappeared."

"Yeah, well, she waltzed into my office late this afternoon."

Shelley stopped slicing to look over at him, and he wondered if she realized just how involved he'd gotten with Janie Doe. "Then she's all right?"

He shrugged. He wouldn't exactly say that. "The case is complicated." That was putting it mildly. "But I can't get it off my mind."

"It? Or her?"

"Both," he admitted with a sheepish grin. That seemed to satisfy her.

"Would you carry this into the living room? Norma called to say they were running a little late."

"I hope they come," Slade said, wondering how badly the chief didn't want to read the letter he'd found.

"Of course they'll come," Shelley said in surprise. "It wouldn't be Christmas without them. Well, Norma, anyway," she added with a laugh. Chief Curtis seemed as fond of Christmas as Slade was.

Shelley put out a tray of snack food while Slade poured them each a glass of wine. With Christmas music playing on the stereo, he helped her decorate the tree. It had become their tradition, since being on their own, to decorate the tree on Christmas Eve, then take it down right after the new year, and always at Shelley's.

The first Christmas after their mother's murder had been the worst, with both parents gone. But the chief and Norma Curtis had helped them start new traditions and Slade had gone along with it for his sister. As far as he was concerned, he could skip the holiday all together and never miss it.

"This is one of my favorites," she said, stopping to

admire a small porcelain Santa. "I remember it from pictures of when we were just babies."

Their mother had loved collecting Christmas ornaments. She could recount where she'd gotten each, many from friends or family, and what year. Each one had special meaning for her.

He watched his sister cradle the Santa in her palm and couldn't help but think about the Santa bell-ringer below his office window earlier. It kept him from thinking about other Christmases—and his mother.

After he'd missed catching the Santa bell-ringer, he'd returned to his office and tried to call Holly Barrows in Pinedale. Of course there was no listing. Why wasn't he surprised? She'd probably made up the name.

Not that he knew what he'd have said even if he'd found a number for her. *I think Santa Claus had my building staked out and I think he was looking for you?* He would sound as crazy as she had.

But he couldn't quit worrying about her. Or worse, worrying that she might be in real trouble—and he hadn't taken her seriously. Between that, and worrying about his mother's letter—and the possible implications of her words, the last thing he wanted to be doing tonight was decorating a Christmas tree. He felt antsy and anxious. Both incidents had shaken him—and during a season when he didn't feel all that grounded anyway.

He and Shelley had just finished decorating the tree when the chief and his wife arrived.

"Slade, get them some wine," Shelley said as she took their coats and shook off the snow. "You must be freezing."

"Nothing like a white Christmas!" Norma exclaimed and moved to the fireplace. ''Oh, your tree is just lovely!''

''Want to help me with the wine?'' Slade asked the police chief pointedly.

Curtis sighed but followed him into the kitchen. Chief Curtis was built like a battering ram, neckless and balding, with a florid complexion, a reputation for being outspoken to the point of being rude and as tough as a rabid pit bull off his chain. Slade knew the chief's bark was worse than his bite, but he still had a healthy respect for the man.

He handed him the letter, then proceeded to fill two glasses with wine, knowing Shelley would get suspicious if they took too long.

''Do we have to do this now?'' Curtis asked, looking down at the yellowed envelope in his hand. ''Damn, Slade, it's Christmas Eve.''

''Roy Vogel didn't kill her. Now I know there was someone else. A man. A secret lover who wanted to remain secret. Maybe at all costs.''

Curtis shook his head. ''You just aren't going to let this go, are you?''

''No. I can't. And considering how my parents felt about you, I wouldn't think you could either.''

Curtis shot him a withering look, then slowly opened the flap and withdrew the handwritten pages. They crackled in his thick fingers as he unfolded them with obvious hesitancy.

''Well?'' Slade demanded when Curtis had finished reading.

''It's vague as hell,'' the cop said with his usual conviction. But Slade noticed that the older man's hands shook a little as he folded the paper, forced the pages back into the envelope and handed it to him. The letter had obviously upset him as much as it had Slade.

"She admitted she'd been secretly meeting someone she didn't want Joe to know about, and she pleaded with Ethel not to give away her secret," Slade said as he put the letter back into his pocket. "What's vague about that?"

"She didn't say she was having an affair," Curtis pointed out, keeping his voice down so the women couldn't hear in the next room.

"I'm going to find out who she'd been meeting," Slade told him as he handed the chief a glass of wine. "Are you going to help me? Someone had to know. Maybe one of her friends. Or her hairdresser. Or the damned meter reader. Someone."

"You're going off half-cocked," Curtis warned. "Even if there was someone, it doesn't mean he killed her."

"There *was* someone. The letter makes that clear. And if Roy Vogel didn't kill her—"

With an oath, Curtis shook his head. "Why did he confess then?"

"Who knows? The guy was always weird and not quite right in the head. But for that very reason, Mom would never have let him into the house, let alone offered him a drink. You do remember the second, half-empty glass on the coffee table?"

"Both glasses had only your mother's fingerprints on them," Curtis pointed out as if he'd said it a million times to Slade. He probably had.

"So the killer wore gloves. It was December. Right before Christmas. It was cold that year. Or he never touched his drink."

Curtis shook his head. "I should never have allowed

you to have a copy of the file. What do you do, dig it out and reread it every night before bed?''

''Don't have to. I know it by heart.'' He didn't tell the chief that he no longer had the file. It was one of the cases the mysterious Holly Barrows, if that was really her name, had stolen, along with a half dozen other older cases. There was no rhyme or reason to the ones she'd taken. None of the cases current—or interesting enough to steal. Probably because the woman was unstable.

''Your father went over that case with a fine-tooth comb. If he'd thought for a moment that Roy Vogel hadn't been guilty—''

''What if he knew about her affair, maybe even knew who it was?'' Slade interrupted. Joe Rawlins had died of a heart attack not six months after his wife's murder. But Joe had never had a bad heart. That's why Slade had always believed it had been heartbreak that had killed him.

Curtis let out an oath. ''You think a cop like your father would let Marcella's murderer go free?''

''Maybe there was a reason Dad didn't go after the real killer. Or couldn't.'' All Slade had was a gut instinct, one that had told him years ago that the wrong man had died for the crime.

Curtis shook his head. ''You're opening up a can of worms here. Have you thought at all about Shelley and what this is going to do to her?''

''I always think of Shelley,'' Slade snapped.

Curtis raised a brow as Shelley called from the other room.

''What's keeping you two? No work! It's Christmas Eve!''

Curtis reached for the glass of wine Slade had

poured for Norma. "Isn't it bad enough that your mother was murdered? You want to murder her reputation as well? And for what? Roy Vogel killed her."

"Then you think she *was* having an affair," Slade said.

Curtis swore. "If she was, I for one don't want to know about it."

Slade fell silent, thinking about what Curtis had said as he followed the chief back into the living room. The conversation turned to the holidays and food and parties.

He stared at the fire, the bright hot flames licking up from the logs, and tried to follow the conversation. But he couldn't quit thinking. About his mother's murder. About the young woman who'd come up to his office. He wondered what she was doing tonight and if she was all right. If she'd ever been all right. And if it was possible she'd given birth to his baby.

He couldn't help but remember in detail how it had been between them and wonder…what if her memory of him were to come back—

He reminded himself that she was a thief and, more than likely, a liar. She'd stolen more than his money and his files. She'd stolen his heart.

Maybe that's why he couldn't get her or the Santa bell-ringer out of his head. Or completely forget about the damned letter in his pocket—and its possible ramifications.

"Don't you think so, Slade?"

He jerked his head up. "What?"

"I asked if you thought this was our best tree yet?" Shelley turned to the others. "Slade and I went out and cut this one ourselves."

He nodded. "The best ever." But he could feel his

sister's worried gaze on him. She knew him too well. It would be hard to keep his concerns from her, let alone the letter. Especially once he started asking around town about their mother.

When Chief Curtis got up to clear the snack dishes, Slade offered to help, following the cop into the kitchen.

"Now what?" Curtis asked, only half as put out as he pretended, Slade suspected.

"Any chance you could get a license plate run for me tonight?"

"Tonight?" the chief asked in disbelief.

"It's for a missing-person case I'm working on." He gave Curtis the license number from the SUV the alleged Holly Barrows had left his office in. "I need a name and address. It's important and I have a feeling it can't wait until after Christmas."

The chief grumbled but stuffed the number in his pocket. "I'll have someone at the DMV call you. *I'm* trying to enjoy the holiday." As annoyed as he sounded, the cop seemed glad that Slade had given up on his investigation into Marcella Rawlins' possible infidelity. At least temporarily.

After all these years, Slade thought, his mother's murder could wait another day. Maybe the woman who called herself Holly Barrows couldn't.

Chapter Three

Christmas Day

The next morning, after opening presents and eating Shelley's famous cranberry waffles with orange syrup, Slade followed the snowplow over the pass to Pinedale. It had snowed off and on throughout the night, leaving the sky a clear crystalline blue and everything else flocked in white with a good foot of new snow on the highway.

Pinedale was a small mountain town, forgotten by the interstate, too far from either Yellowstone or Glacier parks and not unique enough to be a true tourist trap.

He wondered what Holly Barrows was doing here— if indeed the woman he'd met yesterday in his office really was the same Holly Barrows the Department of Motor Vehicles reported lived at 413 Mountain View and drove a blue Ford Explorer.

Pinedale was smaller than Dry Creek, set against a mountainside and surrounded by dense pines. The entire town felt snowed-in and deserted, caught in another time. It had once been a mining camp, some of the scars of its past life still visible on the bluffs around it.

He found Mountain View and drove up to 413. The sign on the lower level of the building read: Impressions Art Gallery. He got out of his truck and glanced in the gallery window, not surprised to see a typical Montana gallery with bronze cowboys and horses, oils and acrylics of Native Americans, and watercolor scenics. He spotted a nice acrylic of a sunny summer scene along a riverbank. The name in the right-hand corner was H. Barrows.

Off to the left of the gallery was an old garage and tracks in the snow where a vehicle had been driven in within the past twenty-four hours.

He stepped back to look up at what he assumed was an apartment on the second floor. The sun glinted on the large upstairs window but not before he'd glimpsed the dark image of a woman there, not before he'd felt a chill.

Rounding the corner of the building, he found a stairway that led up to the apartment. He stopped at the foot of the stairs and glanced around the neighborhood. A handful of kids were dragging shiny new sleds up the side of the mountain a few doors down. A dog barked incessantly at one of the boys. A mother called from a doorway to either the dog or the boy, Slade couldn't tell which. Neither paid any attention.

He didn't see a Santa bell-ringer, but then he hadn't expected to. He figured the man in the Santa suit already knew where to find Holly Barrows. The Santa had been waiting for Holly to show up at Rawlins Investigations as if he'd either feared she would—or had been expecting her. Why was that?

He realized as he glanced up the stairs, that he had more questions than answers. And one big question he needed answered above all the rest. Had Holly given birth to a baby—his baby?

He noticed fresh footprints in the snow on the steps to the apartment. The boot print looked small, like a woman's, and since this was the address Holly Barrows had given as her home on her car registration, he figured the tracks were probably hers and was relieved to see that there was only one set of prints and they ended at the bottom of the stairs.

Someone had come down, it appeared, to get the newspaper and had then gone back up. The newspaper box was empty, the snow on top dislodged. With any luck, Santa hadn't been here and Holly Barrows was home. But was the person he'd glimpsed in the window the woman he was looking for?

He climbed the stairs, finding himself watching the street. The dog was still barking. One of the kids squealed as he and his bright-colored sled careened down the hill and into the street. Kids.

Slade knocked at the door at the top of the stairs and waited, more anxious and apprehensive than he wanted to admit. He expected a complete stranger to open the door, figuring the woman in his office yesterday had lied about everything, although he had no idea why. Maybe she'd borrowed the car. Or even stolen it.

So, when she opened the door, it took him a moment. He stared at her in surprise. And only a little relief. She hadn't lied about her name. Or her occupation. But did that mean she hadn't lied about the rest of it either?

She stood in the doorway, a paintbrush in her hand and a variety of acrylic colors on her denim smock. She wore a sweatshirt and jeans under the smock, but she looked as good in them as she had in the skirt and blouse last night.

"You're the last person I expected to see," she said, not sounding all that enthused about the prospect.

"Yeah." He glanced to the street again, then back at her. "Mind if I come in?"

She opened the door farther, motioning him inside. The place was small, but tastefully furnished, the colors warm and bright, the furniture comfortable-looking. Homey. Except there was no tree. No sign at all that it was Christmas Day.

"Don't you celebrate Christmas?" he asked, curious.

"Not this year."

He followed her through the living area to her studio on the north side of the building. The room, bathed in light, was neat and orderly. He watched her, wondering if the woman he'd come to know this time last year was the true Holly Barrows or if this woman, who seemed to be as dazed as a sleepwalker, was the real one.

She moved around an easel in front of a huge picture window and stopped, seeming startled by what she'd painted.

Not half as startled as he was as he stepped around the easel and saw what she'd been working on. He'd expected something like the idyllic summer scene he'd seen in the gallery downstairs. The two paintings were so different no one would have believed they were done by the same artist.

He stared at the disturbing scene on the canvas, feeling ice-cold inside. He didn't need to ask what the painting depicted. It could have been the birth of Satan, it was so foreboding and sinister. Three horrible crea-

tures with misshapen grotesque faces and dark gowns
huddled at the end of a bed waiting expectantly for the
birth.

While he couldn't see the patient's face in the painting, he could feel her pain and confusion—and fear in
the angle of her body, the disarray of her wild dark
curly hair and the grasping fingers of the one hand
reaching toward the ghouls at the end of the bed, toward her baby.

The painting was powerful and compelling, and
seized at something deep inside him. Sweet heaven.

"We need to talk," he said, even more convinced
of that after seeing what she'd been painting.

She nodded and washed her paintbrush, the liquid in
the jar turning dark and murky as she worked. He
watched her methodically put the brush away, wipe her
hands on the smock, then take it off.

"Why did you wait so long to start looking for your
baby?" he asked.

She looked up, her eyes the same color as the Montana winter sky behind her. "Mr. Rawlins—"

"Slade."

"Slade." She seemed to savor his name in her
mouth for a moment as if she'd tasted it before, then,
frowning, continued as she led him into the living
room. "I believed that my baby had been stillborn. I
had no reason not to." She waited for him to sit, then
perched on the edge of a chair, her hands in her lap.
"I woke in a hospital. The nurse told me. I thought at
first that my belief that the stillborn wasn't my baby
was nothing more than denial. It wasn't until I started
having these memories—if that's really what they
are—" She shook her head. "Before that, I just assumed my sister-in-law was right. That my grief over

losing the baby was causing my...confusion about the birth.''

Sister-in-law? ''You're married?'' he asked, unable to hide his surprise—or dismay.

She shook her head. ''Widowed. My husband died a year ago.'' She looked away. ''Are you going to take my case, Mr. Rawlins?''

He didn't correct her. He was still mulling over the fact that she'd had a husband. And the man had died a year ago. Just before Slade had met her? He felt as if she'd sucker punched him. ''There are a few things I need to know.'' That was putting it mildly.

''I will tell you everything I can.''

An odd answer, he thought, all things considered. ''I'll need you to agree to an examination by a doctor.''

''To prove that I recently delivered a baby.''

He nodded.

She didn't seem offended. ''What else?''

''I'll need the name of your doctor during your pregnancy, and I'll want to talk to the doctor at the hospital who allegedly delivered your baby.''

''I didn't have a doctor during my pregnancy. I was seeing a midwife.''

He lifted a brow at her. She didn't seem like the midwife type. ''Was that your idea?''

She flushed. ''Actually, my sister-in-law suggested her. The woman is highly regarded as one of the top midwives in the country. Her name is Maria Perez. She just happened to have bought a place near here and was on a sabbatical. I was very lucky to get her.''

He stared at her. Something in the way she said it caught his attention. It almost sounded rehearsed. And too convenient. ''You have her number then?''

Holly came up with the number from memory. He wasn't sure why that surprised him either.

"Something else. Why did you drive fifty miles over a mountain pass in a blizzard on Christmas Eve to hire a private investigator?"

"I went to Dry Creek to the last-minute-shoppers art festival at the fairgrounds to look for promising new artists for my gallery. I go every year."

Again, the lines sounded rehearsed. Or as if they weren't her own. Was the art festival where she'd been last year before she'd come stumbling out of the snow and into his headlights?

"Although, this year I almost didn't go," she added with a frown, a clear afterthought.

"So why did you?"

She shook her head. "My sister-in-law thought it would be the best thing for me."

He wondered about this sister-in-law who knew so much. "And do you hire a private investigator every year?" he asked, the sarcasm wasted on her.

"Of course not. I never intended to hire anyone. I was driving by and I saw your sign through the snow and—" She looked up at him and shook her head. "I don't know why I came to you. I just had this sudden need to know the truth and there you were."

"No matter what that truth is?" he had to ask.

"No matter what you discover," she said, but he heard a slight hesitation in her words. She sounded scared and unsure. He couldn't blame her. He felt the same way.

He went for the big one. "What about the father of your baby?"

"I don't see what that has to do—"

"If your baby really was stolen, the father of the baby seems the prime suspect."

It was clear she'd already thought of this. She nodded. "I..." She licked her lips and swallowed. "I don't..."

"You don't know who the father of your baby is?"

"I know what you must be thinking."

He doubted that. "Surely, you have some idea or can at least narrow it down."

"Are you familiar with alcoholic blackouts?"

He stared at her. "You're an alcoholic?" The only thing he'd ever seen her drink was cola.

"Let's just say I don't remember getting pregnant and leave it at that for now."

He studied her for a long moment. Was it possible he knew more about the conception of their baby than she did? "When can you see a doctor?"

Relief washed over her features at his change of subject. "The sooner the better," she said.

"No problem. I think I can get you an appointment this afternoon." Dr. Fred Delaney had delivered both Slade and Shelley and had been a friend of the family for years. He would make time for this, Slade knew. Dr. Delaney was also on his list of people to talk to about his mother. "Is that too soon?"

"No." She rose as he got to his feet.

He considered telling her about the two of them. That after doing the math, he figured the baby had to be his. But first he had to know if there really had been a baby.

He started to leave and stopped. "Last night, when you came to see me at my office..."

"Christmas Eve," she said, then waited for him to go on.

"There was a Santa bell-ringer in front of my building. Maybe you saw him?"

She shook her head, frowning as if wondering what that had to do with anything.

"I think he had my office staked out. I saw him on a cell phone as you were leaving. I think he'd been waiting for you." He saw her pale, her hand trembling as she grasped the back of the chair he'd been sitting in for support.

"Then they know I've come to you," she said, fear making her blue eyes darken.

"They?" he asked, just to clarify.

"The people who took my baby."

The monsters in the painting.

If "they" existed outside this woman's mind.

The Santa bell-ringer, on the other hand, had been real. He described the Santa as best he could, hoping she'd recognize the guy as someone she knew. But while the man hadn't been hiding behind a monster mask—he *had* been hiding under a beard and hat and possibly a whole lot of padding. Like the monsters in her painting, real or not, Santa hadn't wanted to be recognized either, it seemed.

"I can't place him from your description," she said.

He nodded, not surprised. "You just might want to be…careful." He wanted to warn her, but he didn't have any idea against what—or whom. The bottom line was: if those monsters in her painting existed, then Holly Barrows was in danger.

"You don't have a phone?" he asked, remembering that he hadn't found a listing.

"I have it listed under the gallery." She rattled off the number.

He memorized it. "I'll call you with a time. We can meet at the doctor's office."

He glanced back at the painting as he left and almost wished she really *was* crazy. The alternative scared the hell out of him.

DR. FRED DELANEY had grayed in the years since he'd delivered Slade and Shelley. He'd come to Dry Creek right out of medical school and ended up staying. Now in his sixties, he was semi-retired.

"You know my office is closed the week of Christmas," he said when Slade called him.

"That's why I'd like you to see this woman. I'd just as soon have this done…quietly."

Dr. Delaney didn't ask. "Three o'clock."

Holly Barrows arrived a few minutes before her appointment. Slade had half expected her not to show and realized he was going to have to start believing at least some of what she said.

The checkup didn't take long. Dr. Delaney came out of the examining room and motioned for Slade to follow him into his office.

"Close the door," he said as he went around behind his desk.

Slade didn't like the look on the older man's face.

"She delivered a baby in the last month or so. Is that what you wanted to know?"

Sweet heaven. Slade felt light-headed. His baby. Holly had been telling the truth.

"There was quite a lot of tearing," Dr. Delaney continued. "The baby could have been overly large. Either there wasn't time for an episiotomy or…one just wasn't done. I would imagine she was in a lot of pain during the delivery."

Slade felt a cold anger fill him. "You're saying the delivery wasn't handled properly?"

Dr. Delaney blinked. "I would have no way of knowing that. The baby could have come too quickly for anything to be done."

"Or the doctor could have bungled it." Slade knew how doctors hung together. Especially when the word *malpractice* started floating around.

"Do you know who delivered this baby?" Dr. Delaney asked in answer.

He shook his head. Maybe a midwife. Maybe monsters. "But believe me, I intend to find out."

It wasn't until he and Holly left the office that Slade realized he'd forgotten to ask Dr. Delaney about the man in Marcella Rawlins' life.

"Are you all right?" he asked Holly once they were outside.

She looked over at him and he sensed something different about her. She didn't look as much like a sleepwalker. "Did you get the proof you needed?"

"Yes. I'm sorry you had to go through all of that." All of it, including the pregnancy and delivery without him.

"Where to next?" she asked, her eyes glinting with what appeared to be a combination of anger and stubborn resolve. This wasn't easy for her, he could see that. But she wasn't backing down. It reminded him of the Holly Barrows he'd known. And that was something he didn't need to be reminded of.

He hadn't planned to take her with him, but he changed his mind. "The hospital. I want to find out who supposedly delivered your baby."

Dr. Eric Wiltse didn't look anything like a doctor. He wore jeans, a T-shirt and a Carhartt jacket. His face was tanned and his sunbleached hair hadn't even started to gray at the temples. It was pulled back in a ponytail. How he'd ended up in Dry Creek, Slade could only wonder. His office was in the new building at the edge of town but this morning he was making rounds at County Hospital, a small fifteen-bed hospital with an even smaller staff because of the holiday.

"Dr. Wiltse?" Slade inquired, although he'd already seen the man's name tag. He stepped in front of Wiltse, blocking his way.

The doctor, not much older than Slade, seemed more annoyed than surprised as he glanced from Slade to Holly. He didn't seem to recognize her.

"We just need a moment of your time," Slade said, pushing open a supply-room door and shoving the good doctor in.

"Hey, what the—" That was all Dr. Wiltse got out before Slade grabbed a handful of the man's shirt and shoved him against a shelf full of towels.

"I understand you were the emergency-room doctor the night Holly Barrows delivered her baby," Slade said. "I don't have a lot of time and even less patience."

The doctor's eyes widened as he took in Holly again. "This is against all hospital pol—"

"The delivery. Were you assisted? Did you deliver the baby by yourself? If you want, Ms. Barrows here will sign whatever papers you need to release you from any oaths you might have taken, doctor."

"And who will keep me from filing assault charges against you?" the doctor asked, jerking free of Slade's grasp. But he didn't try to leave the supply room. Nor did he look like he was going to put up a fuss.

"I'm sorry, but I don't remember you," he said to

Holly. Memory loss seemed to be going around. "When did you deliver?"

"Halloween night. I was told my baby was stillborn."

His eyes narrowed and he nodded, recollection sparking in his expression. "Yes. You look...different." His gaze came back to Slade's, a hardness to it. "I assume you're the father?"

Slade assumed the same thing, but said nothing.

The doctor continued. "Yes, I remember now. The male infant was stillborn."

A son. Slade felt sick, filled with a terrible sense of loss. The baby had been stillborn. His baby. His baby and Holly's. And, as much as he didn't want to admit it, the sister-in-law had been right. In her grief, Holly had come up with this crazy story about monsters, a secret room and a baby who had lived and was stolen and replaced with a stillborn.

"Then you delivered the baby," Slade said, feeling sick.

The doctor looked surprised as he glanced from Slade to Holly and back again. "She had already given birth when she was brought in, more than likely without any help, from her condition." His look said he thought Slade would have known that. "She was unconscious and suffering from hypothermia. I stitched her up and tried to make her comfortable the best I could."

Slade stared at him. "She didn't give birth here? Then where?"

"I have no idea. I was told that both mother and infant had been found in that condition and some good Samaritan got them to the hospital." His accusing tone made it clear he wondered where the father of the baby had been during the delivery.

Was there even the slimmest chance that Holly's memories could be real? That their baby was still alive somewhere? He tried to hold down the surge of hope, but it was impossible. However, he reminded himself, this still didn't rule out the possibility that Holly had given birth alone for whatever reason. She would have been frightened and in a great deal of pain and then when the baby was stillborn, she would have had a monstrous amount of guilt—as well as tearing.

"This good Samaritan, do you know where we can find him?" Slade asked.

"You would have to ask the admitting nurse. I was called in just to check them both and pronounce..." He glanced at Holly, a practiced look of sympathy coming to his gaze. "...the baby stillborn."

"You're sure it was hers?" Slade said.

The doctor blinked. "Who else's baby would it have been? Both mother and child were covered in blood and it was obvious she'd just given birth."

"Then the umbilical cord was still attached?" Slade asked.

Dr. Wiltse looked uncomfortable. "The cord had been severed, but I assumed the mother had done that herself before she passed out."

"Is that normal—to pass out after a delivery?"

The doctor shrugged. "It's possible. It was also cold that night. She was experiencing some hypothermia."

"Could she have been drugged?"

Dr. Wiltse blinked. "I wouldn't know. We don't routinely check for drug use."

"Is there any way to find out?"

The doctor seemed to consider this for a moment.

"We always do blood typing on both mother and baby, but we only keep the samples for seven days after the birth."

Blood typing. "Would the blood typing confirm the baby was hers?"

"Possibly. It would depend on the blood type of the mother and father compared to that of the baby."

Slade glanced over at Holly. She looked pale and scared. "Where do we find the admitting nurse from that night?" he asked Wiltse. "Also we'll need a copy of the blood typing."

"You might try the front desk," the doctor said, straightening his clothing as he brought himself up to his full height. "It's the novel way we do things around here, rather than in supply closets." He glanced past Slade to Holly. "I'm sorry about your loss."

She nodded, and Slade pushed open the door to let the doctor pass. "Thanks."

At the front desk, Holly asked for a copy of the blood typing on her and the stillborn baby. She filed out a written request form and was told to check back the next day since that office was closed for Christmas.

The nurse on duty didn't want to, but finally agreed to take a look at the admittance sheet from Halloween.

"I remember that night. It was pretty slow early, but then as usual we got real busy," the nurse said, checking the schedule. "Carolyn Gray was the admitting nurse." She checked the admittance sheet. "Nope. It doesn't say anything about who brought in Holly Barrows or her infant. Sorry."

"Is Carolyn Gray working today?" Slade asked.

"Called in sick." There was suspicion in the nurse's tone. But anyone who called in sick for work on Christmas would be suspect.

"It's urgent we speak with her."

It took a little coaxing but they finally got Carolyn Gray's address and phone number. She lived in an apartment house on Cedar and Spruce streets called The West Gate. The nurse at the desk tried Carolyn's home phone number but there was no answer.

"She probably has it unplugged," the nurse said, obviously not believing that any more than Slade did. Except he was hoping for Carolyn Gray's sake that she really was sick.

On the way to The West Gate, he tried Holly's midwife again on his cell phone. He'd been trying all morning with the same result. No answer. He was ready to hang up when a female voice came on the line.

"Maria Perez?"

"No, I'm the caretaker," the woman said.

"The caretaker? Has Ms. Perez left town?"

After a long silence, the woman said, "I'm sorry, but Maria Perez was killed in a car wreck."

He sucked in a breath. "When was that?"

"October. I'm just taking care of the place until the estate is settled."

"Can you tell me when exactly she was killed? Was it on Halloween?"

"No, the day before. Would you like a member of her family to call you?"

"No, that won't be necessary." He clicked off the phone and glanced over at Holly, who was waiting expectantly. "Maria Perez was killed in an automobile accident the day *before* Halloween."

"Then she couldn't have been one of the monsters," she said.

"No." But had someone seen to it that Maria Perez wasn't at the birth?

Holly stared out at the passing town, visibly shaken by the news. He didn't have the heart to tell her what he feared they'd find at Carolyn Gray's apartment.

Chapter Four

The West Gate was about as upscale as Dry Creek got. A half-dozen two-story apartment buildings with bay windows and balconies painted the recent color of choice: tan. Slade idly wondered what kind of money nurses made these days as he and Holly found Carolyn Gray's unit, knocked at the door and waited. To neither of their surprises, Carolyn Gray didn't open the door.

"Keep an eye out," he told Holly as he pulled out his lock-pick kit and went to work on the door. It was a simple lock and Carolyn hadn't set her dead bolt.

"Are you sure about this?" Holly asked with obvious apprehension as he opened the door.

"Carolyn?" he called softly.

No answer.

Holly followed him deeper into the apartment.

He had a bad feeling that Carolyn Gray was probably the only one who'd seen the person who'd brought Holly and the baby to the hospital, especially if most everyone else had been busy that night. If Holly was right about her baby being born alive and then stolen, that person wouldn't want to be identified.

By the time he pushed open the bedroom door, he'd pretty well convinced himself that they'd find Carolyn

Gray murdered. Holly's paranoia was definitely catching. And quite possibly with good reason.

Instead of finding a body though, he found the place had been cleaned out. And in a hurry! Empty drawers hung open, abandoned clothes hangers were piled like pick-up-sticks on the closet floor. Carolyn Gray was gone and it didn't look as if she'd be back. But had she left on her own?

After finding nothing of interest in the apartment, they left.

"There's a chance I'm not crazy, isn't there?" Holly said quietly as she climbed back into his pickup.

"Yeah." A slim chance at this point. But a chance. The same chance that he might now be looking for his own very-alive baby. He didn't want to think what had happened to Carolyn Gray.

"Did you have any tests done while you were pregnant?" he asked, hoping for at least one that might prove the stillborn wasn't hers.

Holly shook her head. "Maria, my midwife, didn't feel it was necessary."

"So you didn't know the sex of your baby?"

"No."

And there were no tests anywhere as proof. How convenient. Other than the blood tests taken at the hospital.

He drove back to Dr. Delaney's office, where they'd left her SUV. "I want to talk to your sister-in-law," he said as he pulled into the parking lot next to her car. "She was there, you said, when you woke up at the hospital. Did you call her? Or did one of the nurses?"

Holly seemed startled by the question. "I don't know. I never even thought to ask."

"I'd like to see your sister-in-law alone, if that's all right with you." He could feel her gaze on him.

"I should tell you that Inez might be difficult."

"You told her you were hiring me?" he asked, wondering if this Inez person was the one who the Santa bell-ringer had been talking to last night.

She shook her head. "I just mentioned to her that I didn't believe the stillborn baby was mine, and that I was concerned about the blanks in my memory. I didn't mention hiring you because I didn't even know myself that I was going to until I did."

"You didn't mention the...monsters?"

She shook her head and looked appalled at the idea. "Can you imagine what Inez would do?"

He couldn't, but obviously she could and it wasn't good.

"I was thinking about your painting," he said. "One of the monsters seemed smaller than the other two. Do you think it's possible it could have been a woman?" He could feel her gaze.

"Yes, that's true, one is smaller." She sounded surprised that he'd noticed. Or surprised that she hadn't.

"But the painting doesn't prove anything. I mean, how can I be sure it's even a real memory?"

She had a point there. But he found it hard to believe anyone could conjure up something like that.

"You aren't thinking it could be Inez, are you?" she asked suddenly. She seemed to find the idea laughable. "When you meet her you'll see why that isn't possible. She can barely get around."

He'd have to take her word for it. Until he met the woman.

"But I do wish now that I'd never said anything to her about any of this." She let out a sigh and he wondered why she'd confided in him about monster memories—and not her sister-in-law. "You have to understand," she said slowly, "Inez is from an older generation and a very conservative family. My getting pregnant only a month after Allan died was considered a family scandal. Inez doesn't want me making it any worse by pursuing what she sees as lunacy brought on by guilt, grief and postpartum depression."

A possible explanation, one Slade himself had definitely considered. But so far they had no idea where Holly had given birth. Or if the baby taken to the hospital with her was actually hers. And the only other person who might know anything had left town in a hurry. Or had been taken out of town. It was enough to make him definitely suspicious.

Holly's story was crazy. It was a leap to think that some other woman had given birth that night at about the same time and close by in order to make the baby switch. Quite the coincidence. Or maybe not. Just like the midwife getting killed in an auto accident the day before Holly gave birth.

"I hope the blood typing will prove that the baby isn't…yours." He'd almost said *ours*. "Otherwise, we might have to have the body exhumed for DNA testing."

She looked shocked—and scared. "Inez will never allow it. She had the infant buried in the family plot. She even named the little boy after her brother, Allan Wellington."

The sister-in-law had named the baby? "Wellington? Not Barrows?"

"Barrows was my maiden name. I never took Allan's name," she said, and looked away from him out the side window at the passing houses. "We were married less than a week. He was older than I was."

Whoa. She married some old guy who died only a week into the marriage? That didn't sound at all like the woman he'd known. But he reminded himself, he'd never expected her to steal his money and files and skip out on him either. So he couldn't rule out the possibility that Holly had married Allan Wellington for his money. He just hoped he didn't find out that she'd offed the guy.

She fell silent as if she wished she hadn't offered as much information as she had. He wondered if she was worried about what he thought—or suspected. Or if the concern he saw in her expression was over the possibility of riling her sister-in-law.

"You always do what your sister-in-law wants?" he had to ask, studying her. The Holly Barrows he'd known before wouldn't have let some old biddy boss her around.

She seemed surprised by the question. "Inez has a way of wearing you down," she admitted, a sadness to her tone as she opened her side of the pickup to get out.

He glanced around to make sure there was no one around her vehicle, not sure who he was looking for. He doubted he'd recognize the Santa bell-ringer without his beard and hat. But there were few people on the streets with most of the stores closed for the day.

"I'll call you later," he said as she got out. He waited until she drove away, his mind racing. Who was this Inez Wellington that she had so much power over Holly? And Allan Wellington, this man Holly had married, why did his name sound familiar? Something told him the marriage hadn't been a happy one. Or maybe he just wanted to believe that.

He picked up his cell phone and dialed Chief L. T. Curtis.

"What do I need to get a body exhumed?"

"This isn't about your—"

"No." Slade had put his mother's murder on the back burner, but hadn't forgotten about it by any means. "It's for a client of mine. She gave birth recently. There is some question as to whether the baby might have been switched and the wrong baby buried."

Curtis was silent for a moment. "It's happened before. Were these babies born at County Hospital?"

"No, it's complicated," Slade said, not really wanting to get into the details or to involve the police at this point. "What would I need for an exhumation?"

"Enough information to talk a judge into giving me a court order."

In other words, proof. The one thing Slade was real short on.

"I assume this is about that plate you needed run?" the chief asked.

"Yeah. I'm getting the blood typing from the hospital tomorrow and I hope it's questionable enough for a court order."

"I thought she didn't give birth at the hospital," Curtis asked.

"No, but she did go there right after the birth and they routinely take both the mother's and baby's blood."

"This is one hell of a time to ask for an exhumation," Curtis noted.

"Yeah," Slade agreed. "I'll check back with you, but meanwhile I'll be at Shelley's. I'm house-sitting until she gets back from her trip to Tobago.'' Shelley'd had the chance to spend the rest of the holiday with some friends on the Caribbean island, and Slade had insisted she go. He felt better having her out of town right now.

"Too bad you didn't go with her," the chief said, and hung up.

Slade shook his head as he clicked off his cell phone, started his pickup and headed for Paradise.

INEZ WELLINGTON lived some thirty miles from Dry Creek in a condominium in a fancy gated community known as Paradise West. Slade had been born and raised in Montana in a time when only a jack-leg log fence—and often not even that—separated the men from the cows. Because of that, he was contemptuous of gated communities and pitied the frightened people who lived behind the bars.

A stoop-shouldered thin woman with a shock of white hair and small dark eyes opened the door. Inez looked to be in her early seventies and had the pinched face of a woman who hadn't got what she wanted out of life. She leaned on a gold-handled cane and eyed him suspiciously.

"Yes?" she said, even though she knew who he was and why he'd come because he'd had to call even to get in the gate.

"I'm Slade Rawlins, the private investigator Holly Barrows hired," he said again, just so there was no misunderstanding.

But from the look of obvious contempt in her gaze, it was clear she knew exactly who he was and why he was there.

"Yes," she said, motioning him in and triple-locking the door behind him. "The only reason I'm bothering to see you at all is for Holly."

Somehow he didn't believe this woman did anything for Holly's benefit. He stood in the small stone foyer. From what he could see of the rest of the condo, the decor was as severe and cold as the woman herself. A few plaques hung on the wall, tributes to one Wellington or another. Obviously a bunch of overachievers.

He couldn't see the Holly Barrows he knew from the two months they'd spent together last year marrying into this family. He couldn't help but be suspicious and wondered just how old Allan Wellington had been.

"I need to ask you a few questions," he said, hoping the old bat would at least offer him a drink.

She pursed her lips as she shuffled past him and into a sitting room, the tip of the cane tapping the floor. She didn't head for the ornate mirrored bar, but took a straight-backed chair and offered him one that looked equally uncomfortable. It was.

"This is such a waste of time and money," she complained as she brushed at her spotless slacks.

"How long have you known Holly Barrows?" he asked, getting right to it. He didn't want to stay here any longer than he had to.

Inez lifted a thin, veined, pale hand from the arm of her chair. "About two years."

"Did you meet her before or after your brother Allan met her?"

She pursed her thin colorless lips, her hand dropping to the arm of the chair. "We met her at a party, I believe, the same night. Did she also tell you they had hoped to have children? Unfortunately, Allan succumbed to a weak heart before he could produce an heir."

An heir. Slade made a mental note to see how much money Holly Barrows had come into after her husband's rather quick demise and was disgusted with himself for his suspicious nature.

"And how old was Allan?" he asked, unable to contain his curiosity any longer.

The old woman stiffened. "Fifty-one."

"You had the same mother and father?"

Her eyes narrowed. "Of course, we did. I was the firstborn. My mother had trouble conceiving. It's one of the reasons Allan dedicated his life to infertility. He was a change-of-life baby, a miracle. Not that it is any of your business."

"I just want to get the lay of the land, so to speak. Holly, is what, twenty-eight? That's quite the age difference."

Inez raised her nose a little higher. "Allan was a very vital fifty-one. Age doesn't always matter if two people are right for each other." She seemed to choke up. "We had no idea there was anything wrong with his heart."

He wondered if Holly had known and mentally kicked himself for suspecting she had. He dropped the subject of age difference, more convinced than ever that Allan and Holly had been anything but "right" for each other. "I take it Allan didn't have any children from an earlier marriage?"

She made a face as if suddenly smelling something unpleasant. "Allan's first love was his career. He was much too busy to even consider marriage, then he met Holly." She made it sound as if Holly had hexed her poor unsuspecting brother. A definite possibility, he thought, as a man who too had been hexed by her.

"You say Allan and Holly met at a party? What party was that?" he asked.

"I can't see what any of this could possibly have to do with your...investigation into the death of Holly's baby," Inez said. "That *is* what this is about, isn't it?"

"Yes," he admitted. "I was just curious."

And it appeared Inez wasn't about to satisfy any more of that curiosity.

"On Halloween night you got a call to go to the hospital," he said. "Who placed that call to you?"

"One of the nurses, I assume. She said she was calling from County Hospital and that Holly had delivered her baby."

"Then she led you to believe Holly had had the baby at the hospital," Slade asked.

"Well, of course she did," Inez snapped. "Where else would she have had the baby?"

"Well, that's the question isn't it? The doctor says she didn't deliver at the hospital. Someone dropped her and the baby off."

"That's ridiculous."

He could see Inez was the type of woman who believed what she wanted and nothing was going to change her mind.

"Did you see Holly the day she had the baby?"

"No, I hadn't seen her for a couple days. But the baby wasn't due for another week or so."

"The baby came early then?" Was it possible the people who had delivered Holly's baby had induced the labor? Especially if they'd planned to take her baby and had known another woman who was about to deliver a stillborn baby?

He knew that sort of thinking was way out there.

But until he found out where Holly had given birth, he had to wonder if anything wasn't possible.

"What difference does any of this make?" Inez demanded. "The baby didn't live. Allan Junior is buried next to his father. There is nothing more to be said about this."

"His father? Allan Junior? But the baby isn't his, right?"

"Playing up to Holly's delusions isn't helping her," Inez continued as if he'd never spoken. "She's come up with this fantasy about another baby out of guilt. She had another man's offspring when she knew how badly poor Allan wanted a child. Of course, she feels guilty."

Slade could see that Inez was doing her best to make Holly feel that way. But as much as he didn't want this old witch to be right, he was also smart enough to know that the other baby, the one Holly thought she remembered, might be nothing more than a guilt-induced fantasy.

But the mystery still remained as to *where* Holly had given birth.

The elderly woman got to her feet with no small effort, signaling that their "meeting" was over. "It's just a case of guilt, grief and postpartum depression for the dearly loved husband she lost and the child she conceived only to appease that loss."

Slade didn't move. *Guilt, grief and postpartum depression.* The exact words Holly had used and in the same order. The words echoed, making his skin crawl.

"What if Holly's right?" he asked quietly. "What if that baby in the ground isn't hers? What if someone has her child?"

"Then good riddance," the old woman snapped, her

face contorting into a mask of meanness. "That baby should never have been conceived in the first place. As far as I'm concerned, it's dead and gone and Holly's licentiousness is buried with it." She took a ragged breath, anger putting two slashes of scarlet into her otherwise gray face. "Nor will I hear of this so-called investigation of yours going any farther. Holly gave birth to a stillborn baby. That's the end of it."

It surprised him, not how she felt about Holly's baby, but that she'd bury the child as Allan Junior in the family plot.

"I'm afraid it isn't up to you," he said slowly getting to his feet. He could see that she wasn't going to take the exhumation well, if it came to that. "If Holly wants to keep looking for her baby then she has that right."

Inez Wellington narrowed her gaze to pinpoints of darkness as she glowered up at him. "I won't see my brother's memory derogated any more than it has been. If Holly continues to behave irrationally, I shall see that she goes back to the sanitarium." She smiled at his surprise. "So she didn't tell you about her breakdown after Allan's death?" She leaned on her cane, a triumphant, self-satisfied look on her pinched face. "Holly committed *herself.* Since she left the doctor's care without a proper release, those commitment papers are still valid." She smiled. "Let me show you out, Mr. Rawlins. Unless you want to see your client locked up indefinitely, you and I won't be crossing paths again."

The intercom buzzed. He saw her glance at her watch, frown, then look at him. The intercom buzzed again. Someone was at the gate.

She walked to the front door, the intercom continuing to buzz, and waited for him. He could see the irritating sound was wearing on her and wondered why she didn't answer it.

Then it struck him: she didn't want him to know who it was!

He stopped to admire one of the commendations on the Wellington wall of fame. Dr. August Wellington had been honored for his work during World War II. How nice.

"Good day, Mr. Rawlins," Inez said pointedly as she opened the door.

"Shouldn't you get that?" The buzzing was getting to him as well. But now he really wanted to know who was at the gate. He waited, pretending to admire another one of the awards.

Glaring, she reached over and hit the intercom. That was the problem with gated communities. The damned guard at the gate.

"Yes?" she demanded.

The loud voice of the overweight guard who'd let Slade in echoed through the entryway. "Dr. O'Brien from Evergreen Institute is down here. He says it's of utmost importance." It was obvious Dr. O'Brien had been giving the guard a hard time from the tone of the man's voice.

"Let him in," Inez snapped, then spun around, no doubt ready to do battle with Slade.

He didn't give her the pleasure. "Good day, *Ms.* Wellington," he said, smiling as he stepped past her through the open doorway.

She slammed the door with a force that knocked the dogwood wreath from the door. Slade didn't bother to pick it up. Let Dr. O'Brien do it. Whoever he was. And what was so urgent? Slade wondered.

As he drove out through Paradise West, he passed a silver BMW coming up the hill too fast. He only glimpsed the man behind the wheel, but he got the impression the good doctor was very upset about something. Was the Evergreen Institute where Holly had been locked up?

Chapter Five

Slade left, thinking how much he'd like to see Inez Wellington locked up indefinitely. But he couldn't shake the terrible feeling that Inez might be right. Holly had been institutionalized? That had to have been right before he met her. Right before she told him she believed someone was trying to kill her.

He felt sick. He'd had doubts before about Holly, about her story, about the two of them. But now...

How could he believe anything Holly had ever told him? Or worse, anything that had happened between them? He felt like a fool. And on top of that, they'd had a baby together. A baby that was now probably buried under another man's name.

Why hadn't Holly mentioned she'd been institutionalized?

All the doubts he'd had about her, along with half a million new ones, flooded him, drowning him. He hadn't realized how badly he'd wanted to believe her. To believe they'd shared a baby and that that baby was alive.

He felt torn and guilty. He'd dropped investigating his mother's murder, not because of the chief's threat, but because of Holly. He'd promised his mother he'd find her killer. It was a promise that had weighed heavily on him all these years. And now he'd discovered a lead, one he wasn't sure he trusted Chief Curtis to follow up on, and he'd bailed out on it to help a woman he couldn't trust, a woman he wasn't sure he'd ever known.

He stopped at the edge of town, trying to think, his head aching. He didn't know who to turn to, who he could trust. Curtis had been like a father to him, but right now Slade didn't trust even him. He couldn't shake the feeling that the chief knew more about Marcella Rawlins's infidelity than he was willing to tell him.

He put his face in his hands, eyes closed, head aching, trying not to think about Holly. But that was like telling himself not to breathe. He knew he should just wash his hands of this case. It was only bound to bring him heartache. It already had.

But if there was even a remote chance that Holly might not be crazy, might be telling the truth— The truth was, he admitted with a curse, he still loved the woman he'd met last Christmas, and, if possible, he wanted to find her again. If she still existed. If she'd ever existed.

He rubbed his hands over his face and sat up. Impulsively, he picked up his cell phone and dialed, determined not to let anything stop him. Dr. Delaney answered on the third ring.

"I'm sorry to bother you again," Slade quickly apologized. "It's about my mother." He could hear Christmas music in the background and faint voices and wished for a moment that he'd had the good sense to wait until after the holidays.

"Yes?" Fred Delaney asked, a slight impatience in his tone.

"I found a new lead in her murder," he said charging ahead blindly. "I think she was seeing someone. A man."

The last words hung in the air for a long moment.

"Marcella?" Delaney asked sounding surprised. "You don't mean having an affair?"

Slade took a breath. "Exactly."

The voices in the background quieted as if whoever was at the house with the doctor was also listening to that end of the conversation. Or maybe Slade just imagined it. The same way he'd imagined the Christmas music playing more softly in the background as if someone had turned it down.

"That doesn't even dignify an answer," Delaney said heatedly. "Obviously you didn't know your mother. Is that all?"

"Yes." It was the only thing he could think to say, surprised by how adamant Delaney had been.

The doctor hung up, the thud of the receiver echoing in Slade's ear.

So much for Dr. Delaney.

He started to put the cell phone down and changed his mind. He'd put this off long enough. He dialed Norma Curtis. She was home, but the chief wasn't. Just as he'd hoped.

"I'm so glad to see you," Norma said when she opened the door. She was a petite woman with snow-white hair, warm brown eyes that always seemed to twinkle, and a round, full face that belied her years.

"I hope you don't mind me stopping by," he said, stomping the snow from his boots.

"You know better than that. I have a pot of coffee

on and I just baked sugar cookies. Would you like some?''

He smiled in answer. He'd never been able to turn down her sugar cookies. She'd gotten the recipe from his mother, and he was pretty sure she purposely always kept a batch around for him and Shelley during the holidays for that very reason.

She poured them each a cup of coffee, then motioned to a chair at the kitchen table. He took the cups of hot coffee over, placed them on the table and pulled out a chair for each of them. She followed with a plate of just-iced cookies.

"I suspect this isn't a social call," she said after he'd downed several cookies and sipped politely at his coffee rather than just jump right in with what he'd come for. "What's on your mind?"

He smiled his thanks. With Norma and the chief, he didn't have to beat around the bush. He appreciated that, since patience wasn't his long suit.

He pulled out his mother's letter and handed it to her. "I would imagine the chief already told you about this."

Norma opened the letter, taking note of who it was from, then read it slowly. When she finished, she carefully folded it and put it back in the envelope, avoiding his gaze.

"You knew," he said, surprised almost beyond words.

"Yes," she said. "I knew."

He could see she had no intention of telling him anything. "I've never believed that Roy Vogel killed my mother."

She nodded.

"This man, whoever he was, I feel it in my gut, he's

the one who killed her. And all these years, he's gotten away with it.''

She swallowed, tears filled her eyes as she looked away.

''If there is even a chance this man did it, don't you want to see him brought to justice? Please, help me. You were my mother's best friend.''

''Oh, Slade.''

He felt as if his heart would burst. ''Then she *was* having an affair?''

Norma looked at him, her gaze full of compassion and pain. ''I don't know that it was an 'affair.''' But the look in her eyes told him otherwise. ''I only saw them once. I stopped by the house. Through the window, I saw her in the arms of a man. I only got a glimpse of him before she spotted me. I hurriedly left.''

Definitely inconclusive evidence, even to him, that his mother had been having an affair. ''That's it?''

''Your mother caught up to me as I was leaving and begged me not to tell anyone.'' She stopped, the words obviously coming hard. ''Especially not your father.''

''You never asked her about him?''

''Never. All I knew was that she met him on Tuesday and Thursday afternoons.''

Tuesdays and Thursdays? The two days of the week that he and Shelley walked to the police station to meet their father and ride home with him. The two days of the week they all came home late.

Slade felt numb. ''Does the chief know?''

She shook her head. ''He wouldn't have believed it anyway.''

''Then he didn't mention this letter to you?'' Slade asked in surprise.

''No, did you expect him to?''

As a matter-of-fact, Slade had. He'd always thought there were no secrets between the chief and Norma.

"Do you have any idea who he might have been?" he asked her. "Any idea at all?"

She shook her head. "I never asked. Your mother never told me. It was better that way."

He wondered if he knew anyone, really *knew* them. "How could my mother live with that sort of deception?" He met Norma's gaze. "How could you?"

She didn't even flinch. He'd expected to see guilt, regret. Instead, her eyes blazed with something he couldn't understand.

"Your mother was happy, happier than I had ever seen her," Norma said with a rush of feeling. "I loved your mother like a sister. I wanted to see her happy."

He couldn't believe what he was hearing. "What about my dad and us kids?"

"I knew she would never leave your father or you kids."

"How do you know that?" Slade demanded.

"She loved him, loved you and Shelley, too much."

He snorted at that. "You don't have an affair if you love your husband."

"Don't you?" she challenged. "Whatever she got from this man, she wasn't getting at home."

He stared at her, shocked by her attitude as much as her words.

"Sometimes a woman needs more than her husband can give her," Norma said. "And I'm not talking about sex."

Slade could only stare at her. "You sound as if you—"

"As if I know firsthand?" She looked away. "It was

a long time ago. I was very young. I wanted children. L.T. was working all the time—

"I don't want to hear this," Slade said, suddenly getting to his feet, sloshing coffee from his cup onto the tablecloth.

"Maybe you *should* hear this. You are so quick to judge your mother."

He felt as if she'd slapped him. "I'm trying to find my mother's killer. That's all." But he knew she'd struck a chord. He'd seen his mother as perfect. Just as he had Norma. He swore under his breath as he sat back down, took a paper napkin and began to sop up the spilled coffee. "It's just such a shock. You think you know someone..."

Norma nodded. "People are human. Sometimes they make mistakes."

"Was *your* affair a mistake?"

"No," she said flatly.

He stared at her. Was she saying marrying L.T. had been her mistake? "Did you ever think about leaving the chief?" he had to ask.

She dropped her gaze in answer.

He was almost too shocked to ask. "What happened to the man?"

"He was in love with someone else."

He shook his head, beyond disillusioned. "You have no idea what my mother would have done. Maybe she was planning to leave us and the man didn't want that." A thought struck him. "Or maybe he was married and my mother threatened to tell his wife. Whatever happened between my mother and this man, it got her killed. I'd stake my life on it."

He looked at Norma, the last person he would have expected to have an affair. No, he thought, his mother was the last person. Norma sat with her hands wrapped around her coffee cup, huddled over the hot dark liquid as if needing the heat. He could see the weight of the deception in her shoulders, the weight of keeping her best friend's secret, of keeping her own. "You never told the chief?"

She shook her head, not looking up. "It would have killed him."

Slade nodded. "I think it killed my father."

As HE DROVE AWAY, Slade thought back to his childhood. His mother always at the stove when he and Shelley came home from school. She seemed always to be cooking. His father was usually late because being a cop wasn't like a desk job.

Had his mother been different on Tuesdays and Thursdays? Not that he could remember. He'd always thought his mother was happy. Had everything been a lie?

Another thought wormed its way in as he drove through town. His father had been a cop. If Joe Rawlins had suspected something, wouldn't he have investigated? What would his father have done if he found out his wife was having an affair?

The thought shook him as he pulled into the visitors parking lot of the Dry Creek Police Department.

"WHY DIDN'T YOU tell me before this just whose family plot you wanted to dig up?" Curtis demanded after Slade told him.

Slade stared dumbly at the chief as he closed the door to the cop's office. "You knew Wellington?"

"Dr. Allan Wellington? Damnation, Slade."

"The baby isn't Allan's. Allan's been dead for over

a year," Slade snapped. He didn't want to talk about Allan Wellington. He didn't even want to think about him. Not now. "And who the hell cares about Allan Wellington anyway?"

"I see," Curtis said in his so-that's-the-way-it-is voice. "Judge Koran will care. And Inez Wellington will care a whole hell of a lot."

"Inez doesn't have to find out." Slade said.

"Judge Koran is a good friend of Inez Wellington's. Need I say more?"

No, Slade thought. It seemed Inez had powerful connections.

Curtis let out a loud sigh as he sat back down behind his desk. "Only you would take a client who was married to Allan Damn Wellington, of all people."

He wondered how Curtis knew who Wellington was when Slade had only a vague feeling he'd heard of him.

"Holly was only married to him for a matter of days. And what did he do anyway, invent a cure for cancer or something?" Slade demanded, taking a seat across from the chief. Why hadn't he even thought to ask Holly what kind of doctor her husband had been? He knew the answer to that one. He didn't like the man. Didn't even have to know anything about him to know that.

"He was just one of *the* top infertility doctors in the U.S.," Curtis said. "He made it possible for *thousands* of couples to have children."

Something in the way he'd added the last— "You and Norma went to him."

The expression on the cop's face hardened. Curtis wouldn't like his wife confiding their secrets. "We were one of the couples he couldn't help. It seems I'm sterile."

Slade heard the bitterness, the disappointment. "I'm sorry."

"I don't want your sympathy," Curtis snapped. "At least I'm not responsible for bringing you into the world."

Slade pulled up a chair and sat down, feeling tired and lost.

"Look, the sister-in-law had the baby named Allan Junior and buried the body in the Wellington family plot."

Curtis lifted a brow. "How did that happen if it wasn't his kid?"

"You'll know when you meet Inez—if you haven't already. Anyway, it turns out that there is a good chance the baby isn't even my client's. But the infant definitely wasn't Allan Wellington's."

"You know that for a fact?"

"For a fact," Slade said meeting his gaze.

The chief let out a long sigh. "The Wellington name means a lot in this country, let alone this area. The doc was like a god. He was on talk shows!"

Slade had heard enough. "Are you saying there isn't any chance of an exhumation if we find we need it to prove the paternity of the baby?"

"We?"

He ignored that. "Well?"

"Wellington's sister will raise holy hell. It won't be easy to get an exhumation. You're going to have to have a damned good reason."

"The baby in that grave could be mine," Slade said. That was the bottom line. "If it's not, then the infant I sired is more than likely on the black market right now. If it hasn't already been sold. Or worse."

Curtis actually seemed at a loss for words. He shook

his head. "Well I'll be damned. This must be that woman you had staying with you this time last year, the one who couldn't remember who she was."

Slade had forgotten that the chief had met Holly. "Yeah." But he hadn't come here to talk about Holly Barrows. He took a breath and let it out slowly. "I just spoke with Norma. She knew about my mother's secret."

The chief looked as if all the wind had been knocked out of him. He got up from behind his desk and went to the window, his back to Slade.

"Norma knew?" he asked, shock and disbelief in his voice. "Does she know who the man was?"

Slade studied the older man from the back, unsure why the cop was taking this so badly. From the beginning, Slade had had a bad feeling that Curtis knew more about this than he was willing to tell him, but never more than at this moment. "She says she doesn't. But I think *you* do."

"Why would you think that?" Curtis asked, his back still to him.

"Gut instinct. Isn't that what you said made a good cop? Isn't that what you told my father all the time?"

The chief didn't answer as he turned slowly around. His face had grayed. He looked older than his years. He moved to his chair and gripped the back, his knuckles white.

"When were you planning to tell me?" Slade asked, fear making his voice sound strangled.

Curtis blinked, then seemed to focus again as if, for a moment, he'd forgotten Slade was there. "You don't think that I was her— Good Lord, don't you know me better than that?"

"I thought I knew my mother better than that,"

Slade snapped. "Now I'm not sure I know anyone. Even you."

"I'm going to say this once and then you and I are never going to have this conversation again, is that understood? I wasn't her lover."

Slade wanted desperately to believe him. Anyone but Chief L. T. Curtis. And yet he'd seen the cop's reaction to the news. If, God forbid, it had been L.T., then what did that do to his theory about his mother's lover being the killer? "Why do I get the feeling that you know who was?"

Curtis shook his head. "Your father was like a brother to me. I would have killed for him."

"Did you?" Slade asked.

"I think you'd better go."

Slade didn't move. "It crossed my mind that one of you could have found out that she was seeing someone every Tuesday and Thursday afternoon. One of you could have been waiting. Or both of you. If you found him with her at the house—" He shook his head. "The two of you—"

"I don't have time for this," the chief snapped as he came around his desk, hitting it with his leg, sending several files showering to the floor. He didn't seem to notice as he started past Slade for the door.

Slade grabbed his sleeve. "L.T.," he said, his voice softening at the name he used to call the chief back when Slade was just a boy. "I have to know the truth. No matter what." The words echoed. So close to what Holly had said.

L. T. Curtis jerked his arm free. His eyes hardened to stone, making it clear he was the chief of police, not the man who'd finished raising Slade. "I've reopened your mother's murder investigation based on the new evidence. It's out of your hands now. Don't butt heads with me on this. I could have your license pulled. And I will.'' He strode to his office door, jerked it open and stomped out.

Slade stared after the man, shaken. The chief had reopened the investigation? Because he now believed that the killer could have been Marcella Rawlins's lover? Or because he wanted to keep Slade from finding out the truth by making the case off-limits?

He started to leave, but bent to pick up the files first. He couldn't miss the photos that had fallen out of one of the files. A half-dozen snapshots of a murder scene. The chief must have been looking at Slade's mother's file when he came in. No wonder the man was worked up.

Agonized, he flipped through the photos, stopping on the last one. A close-up of his mother's hand holding the Christmas ornament she'd pulled from the tree, the last act of her life.

He stared at the tiny golden twin angels. He'd forgotten which ornament she'd grabbed. He'd always just thought she'd been clutching at the tree. But as he looked at the ornament he wondered if she could have possibly been trying to leave them a message.

Twin angels. Wasn't that what she'd always called him and Shelley? Maybe she *had* been trying to tell them something. That she was thinking of him and Shelley, that they were her last thought.

Or maybe she'd just been clutching at anything she could get her hands on—just as he was now.

Chapter Six

As Slade drove toward Pinedale and Holly's studio, the afternoon sun cast long gray shadows across the snow. He could feel the temperature dropping outside the pickup, the windows trying to frost up. He kicked up the heat, his heart heavy, mind racing.

He didn't know what to think. Or who to believe. Nothing had been as it appeared. And now he was doubting people he'd known his whole life.

He pulled up in front of Holly's place, cut the engine and stared up at the apartment, the dying light shining on the window like a two-way mirror. He felt sick with worry and couldn't tell which case had filled him with such dread. Maybe both. His mother's murder pulled at him. Just as everything Inez had told him about Holly did. He feared what Holly would tell him when he confronted her. Feared what he'd find out about his mother.

But, like Holly, he had to know the truth. No matter what. And there was no turning back now for either of them.

For a few minutes, he sat in his pickup, immobilized by a terrible foreboding. Then, slowly, he opened the door and stepped out, not bothering to zip his ski jacket against the bite of the icy breeze. The sun had set, leaving the eastern sky a cold, clear blue. By morning, everything would be covered in thick frost. Or snow. Again.

He thought about the fireplace at Shelley's and about sitting in front of it drinking a glass of Scotch, just staring into the flames. He wanted to forget about everything, just for a little while.

But he couldn't. Not until he talked to Holly. He tried not to think about the baby. The one buried in the Wellington family plot as Allan Junior. Or the one Holly claimed was alive and taken by three monsters in masks.

His steps heavy as he climbed the stairs to her apartment, he felt a weight, like a premonition of bad things to come. For the first time, he wondered if the chief wasn't right. Maybe he didn't want to know who'd killed his mother. Or the truth about Holly Barrows, either.

But he'd opened Pandora's box, and he couldn't close it until he knew what was inside. It was a character flaw, his inability to leave things unfinished. His mother's murder was one of them. Holly Barrows was the other.

Holly gave him a faint worried smile as she let him in. "So you met Inez."

He wanted to ask her what had possessed her to marry into a family like that. But he feared he already knew. "I need you to tell me about your husband's insurance policy. And your breakdown."

She winced and turned back toward the living room. "I would imagine you could use a drink."

He watched her sort through the bottles of liquor in a small bar against the wall, passing up several differ-

ent Scotches to pull out a bottle of Glenlivet and pour
him a couple of inches. Straight. No ice. She poured
herself a cola on ice.

"How did you know I drink Glenlivet?" he asked
when she handed him his drink.

She seemed startled by the question. "I'm sorry, I
should have asked. I just assumed—"

"—that all private eyes drink that brand?"

She dropped into one of the wingback chairs, the
glass in her hand shaking. She looked scared. He knew
the feeling.

"I don't know why I do half the things I do, if you
want to know the truth." Her voice broke as she
glanced up at him, tears in her eyes. "I'm sure you
wonder why I married a man twenty-three years my
senior. I wish I could tell you." She dropped her gaze,
took a drink and licked her lips before looking at him
again.

"I wish I could tell you a lot of things." This time
she met his gaze unflinchingly, reminding him of the
woman he'd known a year ago, making him remember
the feel of her lips on his mouth, on his skin. Holly
had been scared last year, convinced someone was trying to kill her. But there had been a strength of will
about her that he'd admired. She'd had no intention of
giving up without a fight.

This was the first time he'd seen it in this Holly. It
stirred all the old feelings and some new ones. This
was the kind of woman he could fall in love with. *Had*
fallen in love with.

"I have blank spaces in my memory," she said, even
her voice sounded stronger, more determined. "Some
are only for a few hours. Others...are for...longer. I
married Allan after one of those blanks. To answer

your question, my husband left me well off financially. But that wasn't the reason I married him.''

"Inez said you and Allan were trying to have a baby, an heir.''

She jerked back, startled, her gaze nothing short of shocked. "She told you that?''

"Was it a secret?'' he asked.

"No, it's just...not...true. Allan and I never—'' She waved a hand through the air. "—consummated the marriage. Allan had no interest in...any of that.''

Slade stared at her, more than a little confused. "Then why did he marry you? I mean—''

"I know what you mean. To be truthful, I have no idea how we got together or why.'' She smiled ruefully. "I've never admitted that before. At least not aloud. I can't explain why I've done a lot of things I've done in the last year.''

He held her gaze, debating whether to tell her he was one of the "things'' she'd done.

"I didn't marry him for his money, if that's what you're thinking,'' she said.

"How long have you had these...lapses in memory?'' he asked, not about to touch the other.

She looked as if she wasn't quite ready to drop the other subject, but then sighed and said, "They started a little over a year ago.''

"About the time you met Allan?'' he guessed.

"Yes,'' she said, frowning. "I guess it was.''

He could think of a variety of causes for memory loss. Epilepsy. Alcohol blackouts. Multiple personality disorder. Head trauma. Psychosomatic amnesia.

But he'd always been suspicious of coincidence. And it was one hell of a coincidence that Holly's memory loss had started about the time she'd met Allan and his sister Inez.

"Have you seen a doctor about it?"

She nodded. "Dozens of specialists, including Dr. Parris at Evergreen Institute. They all say the same thing. There is nothing *physically* wrong with me. That leaves Inez's theory that I make up the memory losses to cover things I've done that I'm ashamed of."

He wondered if she was ashamed of what she'd done with him. "Evergreen Institute?" Where the upset Dr. O'Brien visiting Inez earlier had been from. "Is that the sanitarium you were committed to?"

"Yes, Inez talked me into it." She let out a humorless laugh. "My so-called breakdown was nothing more than relief. And regret that I'd ever married Allan in the first place. And, of course, confusion because of the memory loss."

"Did you ever see a Dr. O'Brien at Evergreen?"

"No," she said. "He must be new."

Slade had hoped for a tie-in. No such luck. Other than the one common denominator: Evergreen.

Holly seemed upset. "Inez believed Allan and I were trying to have an heir?"

He nodded, watching her closely.

"Well, he got his heir, didn't he?" she said.

"But it's not his baby."

"No. But it also doesn't seem to make any difference to her. Does that make any sense at all?"

"No." He was glad she'd noticed. If she'd been crazy, she wouldn't have noticed, right? He studied her, wondering if she didn't seem a little less blank this evening. "You told Dr. Parris at Evergreen Institute about your memory loss?"

"Of course. It had only just begun then, and Dr.

Parris assured me it was probably caused by the trauma of losing my husband so soon after the marriage.'' She looked up at Slade. ''I knew it wasn't that. But I had lost my mother just six months before that. My father died when I was nineteen, so my mother was the only family I had.''

''I know what it's like to lose your parents,'' he said. ''I lost my mother when I was twelve, and my father not quite a year later.''

''I'm sorry.'' She looked down at her hands clutched in her lap.

''Did the stay at Evergreen help?'' he asked, suspecting he'd met her last year about the time she'd left the place—and according to Inez, without properly signing herself out. Interesting.

''Not really.''

''Why did you leave without checking out of the place?'' Slade asked.

She frowned. ''I don't know. It's odd that I would run away from there. Evergreen Institute is really more like a fancy spa than a sanitarium. I mostly just slept and read and rested.''

He was glad to hear that. He'd been imagining an asylum with padded cells and straitjackets and screams in the night. He worried that when Holly found out about their past, it might send her back there.

''But I don't remember leaving Evergreen—or how or why.''

''Inez made it pretty clear how she felt about your pregnancy,'' he said, still wondering what hold the older woman had over Holly.

''My pregnancy was none of her business,'' Holly replied hotly. ''I'm not ashamed of anything. Least of all that. I should never have told her that I didn't think that baby at the hospital was mine. Or about the memory loss. She's afraid people will think I'm crazy. But maybe I am crazy.''

"Do *you* think you're crazy?"

She hesitated, but only for a second. "No. I think.... I don't know what to think."

He doubted that. She had a theory, she just wasn't ready to voice it, probably because it was so off-the-wall. Nor was he sure he was ready to hear it.

"Has your memory ever come back after one of these blanks before?"

She shook her head. "Only the birth of my baby. If it's really a memory."

But she had remembered something else. She'd remembered that he drank Glenlivet Scotch straight. It was a small thing, but it made him wonder if her memory wasn't coming back and that was why she'd come to him. Again. He hoped to hell he was right.

But the question was, what had caused her memory loss in the first place?

"How long do these memory lapses last?" he asked.

She shrugged. "They vary. Usually I just sense holes in my memory. Time has passed but I can't remember what happened during that time—obviously something when you realize you're pregnant and yet can't remember even meeting a man, let alone...." She looked away, seeming embarrassed. "That's why it's so hard for me to believe that the memories of the birth were real. I'd never remembered anything, not even vaguely."

"Maybe it was the trauma that caused you to remember," he suggested, wanting to believe something was spurring the return of her memory.

"Or maybe it was love? I wanted this baby more than anything. I'm sure that seems odd to you, considering that I don't know who the baby's father is. But while I can remember nothing of those missing months, I have a good feeling about the man who—'' She broke off and took a drink of her cola.

She had a good feeling about him? Is that why subconsciously she'd known to hire him to find the baby? Their baby?

Or was she pulling his string? The thought had crossed his mind, especially in light of the day he'd had. He didn't trust anyone. He was even beginning to question his own instincts.

''I don't know what is real anymore,'' she said, sounding close to tears as she got up to refill his glass. He hadn't even realized he'd drained it. ''Just that I have to find my baby. And save her.''

He watched her go to the bar again, wondering what she had to save her baby from. And knew she had to be wondering the same thing. He started. ''Her?''

Holly didn't respond.

He watched her turn. Her eyes were vacant, her face ashen. ''Holly?''

He'd known a boy in school who was epileptic. Rather than seizures, he had lapses where he would just zone out for short periods of time. Looking at Holly now, he was reminded of that boy.

''Holly?''

She blinked, her eyes luminous and filled with fear as her gaze came back into focus. ''I said her,'' she whispered, sounding scared. ''Oh, I remember her.''

He waited, almost afraid of what she'd say.

''During the delivery, something was wrong. They were rushing around, frantic. I tried to see what was going on. I thought something was wrong with my baby.'' Tears welled in her eyes. ''One of them left the room. When the door opened, I heard another woman, another patient. She sounded as if she was in labor.''

She looked down at the glass of Glenlivet in her hand as if she couldn't remember how it got there, then handed it to him. But instead of returning to her chair and her cola, she walked into the studio.

He sat for a moment, not sure if he should follow her. To his surprise, she returned a moment later, carrying a large canvas. He knew without seeing the painted side what it was. He could tell by the way she held it, the way she frowned down at the work in her hands.

"That's why I believed the room was sound-proofed," she said more to herself than to him as she propped the painting against the wall and moved back to stare at it.

The light cast an eerie glow over the acrylic monsters huddled around the delivery-room scene. He was filled with even more dread each time he saw the work. There was something so raw about the paint slashes, so chilling. He felt a cold draft move through the room.

The three monsters were huddled together, hunched over, waiting with obvious anticipation, making it hard to distinguish their shapes beneath the garb they wore. They could have been men. Or women. Or just figments of Holly Barrows's nightmarish imagination.

"I remember being scared," she continued in a hushed voice as if the walls might be listening, her gaze on that damned painting. "Something was wrong with my delivery. Or my baby." She glanced back at him, no doubt knowing what he was thinking. That all of these images could amount to nothing more than what Inez Wellington believed they did.

"I must have blanked out again. I woke to the sound

of a baby crying,'' she said slowly as if the memory was playing out in her head. ''I opened my eyes. My baby was lying on a small table near my bed. She was kicking her legs.'' Holly turned back to him. If she was putting all of this on, she was one damned good actress. She must have seen his skepticism though.

''I *saw* her,'' she whispered fiercely. ''She was close enough I could see her birthmark.''

He felt a chill. ''A birthmark?''

She nodded, her gaze still glazed as if focusing inward. ''It was heart-shaped and on the calf of her right leg and…she had this little dimple in her cheek.'' She blinked. ''How could I remember something like that if it wasn't real?'' There was a pleading in her tone. ''How is that possible to see something so clearly, if it never happened? My baby was a little girl—not a boy—and she was alive. I saw her!''

A heart-shaped birthmark and dimples. He stared at her, his pulse pounding in his ears. The dimples were genetic; he knew that well enough. But a birthmark?

Shivering, he reached up to rub the back of his neck, suddenly anxious to leave. But he couldn't leave without Holly. He wasn't sure what was going on. And he had no proof that anyone was after her. No more than he'd had this time last year. All he knew was that he didn't feel safe. And neither should she.

''I don't think you should stay here alone,'' he said, wondering how he could convince her.

She looked at him in surprise. ''You're starting to believe me, aren't you?''

What did he believe? That she'd given birth to their baby? That monsters had stolen the baby? That the baby had dimples and a birthmark just like his twin sister Shelley's? And that Holly Barrows was starting to remember, not only the delivery but—him?

"Yeah," he said as he got to his feet and walked to the window. Parting the curtains, he looked out into the empty street. He believed that the Santa on the street below his office on Christmas Eve had reported to someone that Holly Barrows's memory was returning. That meant he also believed that someone had tried to get Holly to forget.

Not that what he believed mattered in the least. Because what the hell did he know? But he wanted to help her. How much assistance she needed was still debatable. All he knew was that he'd have a better chance of helping her if the monsters in the painting were real than if they were in her head. And if the monsters were real, then he had to find their baby— and fast. Too much time had already been lost.

He tried not to think about it. The whole thing scared the hell out of him. Because it was so far out there. And because it didn't make any sense. If the specialists couldn't find any physical reason for her memory lapses, then that left psychological causes.

And that opened up a whole can of worms. The woman he'd met a year ago certainly had been different from this one. But a whole different personality? He didn't buy it.

"Look, let's say you're right and these...monsters stole your baby," he said carefully. "If they find out you're starting to remember the delivery—and them— well, I'd just feel better if you weren't alone right now."

She seemed to study him. "You think I should go stay with my sister-in-law?"

God, no. That couldn't be good for anyone. He

didn't like the fact that Inez had talked her into committing herself. Holly seemed too smart for that. He wondered again what hold Inez had over her. "No. I think you should come stay with me."

He had so many questions, but he figured she didn't have any more answers than he did. And the questions could wait until he got her to Shelley's. He parted the curtains again, taking one last look out the window. The street was still empty, the sky clear and cold, making the fallen snow glow.

As he turned from the window, he heard a sound. "What are you doing?" he demanded, surprised by the intensity in his voice.

She jumped and almost dropped the glass of cola in her hand, the small plastic container in the other. "I was just going to take my pill."

He stepped to her and took the container. "Where did you get these?"

"It's an old prescription that Allan wrote for me. Inez had it refilled...."

He read the label. Xanax. The name of the drug meant nothing to him. No big surprise considering he never took anything stronger than aspirin and was unfamiliar with prescription drugs. "What are they for?"

"They relax me and make me feel better."

"What happens if you don't take them?"

She stared at him in obvious surprise. "I don't know. I—" She looked at the pill she'd spilled into her hand just before he'd stopped her. "Yesterday, I forgot the pills here at the house. Obviously they don't help my memory." She tried to laugh at her joke but instead tears welled up in her eyes.

He removed the baby-blue oblong pill from her hand, putting it back into the container and snapping the lid shut again. "I'd like to have a pharmacist take a look at these before you take any more."

She nodded, her eyes large and scared. "You don't think the pills—?" She picked up her cola and took a drink, her hands trembling.

"I don't know. Maybe I'm just being paranoid but I'd feel better if you didn't take them until I can have someone check them out—" He stopped. She was crying softly. "I'm sorry if I upset you."

"No," she said, hurriedly wiping at her tears. "You haven't upset me. Just the opposite. I can't tell you what it means to have someone believe me." She forced a smile. "Your paranoia is such a comfort, since for so long all I've had is my own."

He started to reach for her, to drag her from her chair and into his arms to hold her and comfort her as he would have a year ago. But he stopped himself, reminded that she didn't know him. Didn't remember the intimacies they'd shared. He was a stranger to her. A stranger who knew every curve, every hollow, every inch of her.

But she didn't know that either.

And it was that secret between them that made him walk to the window instead and look out again, rather than try to comfort her. He could more easily have comforted a total stranger than he could have Holly Barrows at that moment.

"Your gallery is closed for the holiday, right?" he asked, his back to her.

"Yes?"

"We'll go to my sister's. She has a large house with lots of room. She's going to be out of town until after the New Year." He wouldn't be putting Shelley in danger. The house had a good security system, unlike his apartment. And Shelley kept the freezer stocked.

He turned when she didn't answer and saw her look around her home, her studio, as if assessing how she could leave it, let alone go with a man she had only met a night before. A man she had little reason to trust.

He followed her gaze to the painting again. If anything, it was more frightening—and convincing—than when he'd first seen it.

"I think you'd better bring that along." He didn't want anyone else seeing the canvas. Especially the ghouls in the painting. If they existed. If she was really remembering them, it was best they didn't know to what extent.

Holly still hadn't moved, he realized. She sat, holding her glass in both hands, her gaze finally coming back to it and the dark liquid. "I have to ask you something. I don't mean to sound ungrateful. Or suspicious, but why *do* you believe me?"

It was obvious she was having some doubts about coming with him. He'd hoped she would remember the two of them on her own. But he didn't have the time to wait for that now. He wanted out of here. He wanted her out of here.

"Do you recall where you were this time last year?" he asked. "From Christmas Eve through February twenty-sixth?"

Her head jerked up. She said nothing as her surprised gaze locked with his, but her face paled, and she gripped the glass, her hands shaking.

"My twin sister Shelley has a birthmark exactly like the one you described." He reached down and pulled up his pant leg. "So do I. And we both have the Rawlins' dimples."

She dropped the glass. It hit the hardwood floor, shattering like a gunshot, ice shooting out across the hardwood floor, the last of the cola puddling at her feet. But she didn't move. She stared at him as if seeing a ghost. No doubt the ghost of Christmas past.

Chapter Seven

Holly stared at him dumbstruck. *"You?"* she cried, all the ramifications coming at mach-two speed.

He nodded.

"The baby?" If she'd really been with this man from Christmas Eve through February twenty-sixth then— "It's *ours?*"

"So it seems." He didn't sound pleased about that. But who could blame him?

Her head swam. She gripped the arms of the chair trying to still the trembling in her hands, in her body. "I hired you not knowing you were the man who— How is that possible?" she asked, her voice barely a whisper.

"I'd like to think you remembered me. Remembered…us."

Her gaze flew up to meet his. Heat rushed through her. This man *knew* her. Intimately. Her face flamed and she dropped her gaze. "I don't know what to say to you."

"You don't have to say anything," he said easily, his voice deep and almost familiar.

She felt a chill as something like a memory skittered across her bare skin. Fingers, warm, soothing, search-

ing. Bodies welded together with desire and sweat—
She looked away, shocked. It couldn't have been a
memory. Couldn't have been her.

"How did we meet?" she asked, almost afraid to
hear it for fear he'd picked her up in some bar. Or
worse.

She stole a glance at him and reminded herself that
she'd had a good feeling about the man who'd fathered
her baby. Then she listened as he recounted a story
about a woman coming out of a storm on Christmas
Eve a year ago, how his pickup had almost hit her, and
when he'd jumped out of his truck, he'd found her
lying in the snow with no knowledge of who she was—
just the conviction that someone was trying to kill her.

Holly closed her eyes. How could she have spent all
that time with him and not remember? "And I was
with you from Christmas Eve through February twenty-
sixth?"

"Yes."

She took a breath. "We slept together."

"We were lovers," he said softly.

She opened her eyes. "Then it wasn't..."

"A one-night stand? Hardly." His gaze hardened.
"We were in love."

The words reverberated through her. In love? She
couldn't have been more surprised if he'd said he'd
bought her from a wagonload of roving gypsies.

He must have seen her surprise. His jaw tightened,
eyes narrowing, and she realized she'd hurt him. "I
was trying to find out who you were, but you seemed
to have been dropped from the sky. Then I turned my
back one day and you were gone with two hundred
dollars of my money and some files from my office."

She stared at him, horrified. First she'd fallen into

bed with this man, convinced him she loved him, then stolen from him like a common thief? Tears burned her eyes. Maybe Inez was right. Maybe she forgot because of the horrible things she'd done. Or maybe none of this was true. Just as the baby the nurse had handed her at the hospital hadn't been hers.

"Excuse me if I find this hard to believe...." She wouldn't have believed anything he'd told her and would have called him a liar to his face, but he knew the exact dates of the days she'd lost. And there was the baby. Not to mention that flash, that image of the two of them, bodies locked in passion. It had felt like more than a memory as if the image was somehow branded not only in her brain, but on her skin. And there was the birthmark, the dimples.

And yet, she trusted none of it. "If we were in love, why would I steal from you and leave?" she challenged.

He shook his head, his gaze never leaving her face. "I was hoping you'd tell *me* that."

She heard the bitterness in his voice. It was obvious he didn't trust her. Why should he? She'd hurt him. No, not her. "I don't know this other women you say you met this time last year."

"Unless you have a twin sister..."

"I'm sure you know I don't," she said, then continued with her train of thought. "Nor can I imagine doing the things you say I've done."

"Can't you?" he asked, his gaze refuting her claim. She felt herself blush under the heat of it.

"Then explain why you came to me again on Christmas Eve," he demanded. "Why you came to me for help a second time."

"I can't explain it," she said. "I just had this feeling

I *had* to hire you. I'm not sure any more what decisions are mine and which are—'' She stopped, afraid to voice the fear that had haunted her for so long.

He was watching her, waiting.

She swallowed, realizing she had nothing to lose at this point. ''I feel as if someone is…making me do things, things I normally wouldn't do, things I can't even imagine doing, and then wiping the memory from my mind.''

''Things you regret?''

''Yes,'' she said, then added quickly, ''Not everything. Not the baby. Not—'' She waved a hand through the air. ''I just need to remember, to understand what has been happening to me.'' She fought back tears, hating the need to cry. Crying had done nothing to relieve the pain. Or to help.

She rubbed at her eyes and looked away from him, the doubts haunting her. She needed her pill. The thought surprised her. ''The thing is, why would anyone go to the trouble of…making me do *anything?*'' she asked, more to herself than him. ''What could they possibly have to gain?''

''A baby.''

She turned to blink at him. ''All of this for a baby?'' she asked, incredulous.

He shrugged. ''What else have they gained? It wouldn't be the first time somebody wanted a baby so desperately that they did something…heinous.''

''Why my…our baby?'' Her voice broke.

He shook his head. ''It doesn't make any more sense to me than it does you. If someone wanted a baby that badly, they could hire a surrogate. Or adopt. Or just steal an infant from a shopping cart at the grocery store.''

She shuddered at the thought. And yet her baby had been stolen by monsters and she'd seen it happen. Or had she?

"You think it's possible then?" she asked.

"That someone is manipulating you?"

She nodded.

"I think anything is possible at this point."

She felt a wave of relief wash over her. Followed by a jolt of sudden fear. "But what if—" She stopped, realizing what she was going to say as she remembered the feeling she'd had driving by his office Christmas Eve. She'd felt as if she *had* to stop and hire him. Did that mean that she trusted him? That subconsciously, she'd known to go to him again because he was the one person who would help her?

Or had the feeling been *too* strong? Almost as if she didn't have a mind of her own? Almost as if someone had sent her to him?

The thought hit too close to what she'd come to suspect.

"Did anyone try to kill me while I was with you?" she asked, afraid she already knew the answer.

"No."

"Or try to find me?"

He frowned. "No."

"Didn't you find that strange?"

He seemed to study her. "Not at the time. I'm pretty good at what I do."

She suspected he was. But maybe he didn't realize who he was dealing with. Possibly, *what* he was dealing with.

"What if you were set up?" she asked. "*We* were set up? I could have been sent to you. Just as I might have been again this Christmas Eve."

"Nice present," he said with a lift of his brow.

"I'm serious. I felt as if I *had* to contact you." She swallowed, the words sounding ludicrous even to her ears and yet they'd been words she'd said over and over again in her mind. "I'm not sure they aren't controlling me right now and there is nothing I can do to stop them."

"I think you're wrong about that," he said, surprising her. "I think you're starting to remember." He sounded so calm and rational. "First you remembered our baby. Then that Scotch you served me tonight. You picked the brand I drink. You had no way of knowing that except to have remembered it."

She stared at him, wanting desperately to grab hold of any line of hope he threw her.

"I think you're starting to remember me," he continued, his gaze as soft as his voice. "Remembering us. And that's why you came to me. Again."

She smiled in spite of herself. "I like your theory better than mine."

He returned her smile. He had a nice smile. Oh, how she wished she could remember him. Desperately wished it. Because he was asking her to put her trust in him, to put her life in his hands. And she knew if he was the enemy, then he was the worst possible one she could imagine. The father of her baby. A man who knew her better than she knew herself.

"Why didn't you tell me yesterday who you were?" She hadn't meant to make it sound so much like an accusation.

"You weren't ready to hear it yet," he said matter-of-factly.

She watched him go to the window to pull back the

curtain a fraction of an inch and look out, wondering what he was looking for, worse, what he was thinking.

"I hate to imagine what you must think of me," she said. "I stole from you." She knew that was the least of it.

"You and I spent over two months together," he said without turning around. "I got to know you pretty well."

Even without the flashes of possible memory, she could well imagine, since their liaison had ended in a pregnancy. "How is that possible when *I* didn't even know me?"

He turned to look at her, his gaze softening. "The woman I knew was kind, generous, funny, smart, strong, brave, and…very…" The intensity of his gaze could have burned her. "…passionate."

He'd just described a stranger. In her twenty-eight years, she'd never known passion. And yet when she looked into his eyes, she felt something. Just as she had when she'd thought she'd envisioned the two of them locked in each other's arms.

She watched his features soften, a hint of a smile turning up the corners of his lips. "I liked you a lot, all things considered," he said, lightening his tone.

"All things considered?"

"Considering you had no past and thought someone was trying to kill you."

She let out a rueful laugh, still not sure she dared believe him. "I must have made for a fun date."

"Yeah, you were," he said. "Come on. Let's get your things together. Whatever is going on, I'll feel a whole lot safer away from here."

Unsteadily, she got to her feet, avoiding the broken glass and spilled cola. Was he just being protective?

Or did he really believe her? "The more I learn, the more I think I *am* crazy."

"Well, I'm becoming more convinced that you aren't," he said. "Here, let me get that." He went to the kitchen and came back with a broom, dustpan and towel. "Once we get the blood typing results from the hospital lab—"

"We might not have to exhume the body?" she asked, her voice full of hope.

He nodded as he finished cleaning up her spilled cola.

Then Inez might not have to know. Otherwise…otherwise, what would Inez do? What could she do? And why did the thought scare Holly so much?

"Inez can't stop the exhumation if it comes to that," he said, as if reading her mind. "This baby isn't related to her either way." He glanced up. "You should know, your sister-in-law has threatened to see you institutionalized again if you don't drop this."

"I guess I shouldn't be surprised. I warned you about her."

"Inez doesn't scare me."

But she should, Holly thought with a shudder.

"I guess we'll find out just how powerful your sister-in-law is," he said. "Hurry and pack. I want to get out of here."

She went to her bedroom and pulled out her suitcase, her mind racing. Doubts overwhelmed her as she packed. But she thought of her baby. If she hoped to get her little girl back, she knew she needed all the help she could get. And she *had* to believe in someone. Mostly, she was sick of being scared. She wanted to be that woman Slade had described, strong and brave.

She took a deep breath. Maybe she *was* starting to

remember. Maybe Slade Rawlins was proof of it. He had the same birthmark—and the dimples. He drank Glenlivet and somehow she'd known that. And, more important, he seemed to believe her.

She realized how desperately she wanted to trust him. He gave her hope that they would find their baby and finally still the ache inside her. Hope that they would stop whoever was behind this and end the lapses in her memory, the fear for her sanity.

And yet, she knew it could all be a trap. If she was right, if someone had been messing with her mind— If that were true, couldn't they have programmed her to do exactly what she was doing at this moment— packing to go with Slade?

She fought that horrible thought. No, she'd started to remember, and that's why the monsters had had the Santa bell-ringer outside Slade's office. They were afraid her memory was coming back, and that when that happened, she would go to Slade.

But now the monsters knew she'd done just that. They would try to stop her. And what better way than to use Slade to do it? a voice inside her head taunted. To pretend her baby had been his? To pretend they had been lovers? To pretend he was taking her some place safe?

She froze at the thought, a silk blouse in her hands. She brought the cool cloth to her face, fighting back tears. What if Slade was one of them? Wasn't that her greatest fear? That he would give her hope, then snatch it away?

"Are you all right?" he asked from the doorway.

She turned, startled, and nodded slowly.

He moved to her in two long strides and, taking the blouse from her fingers, folded it into the suitcase.

"We can buy you more clothes if you need them," he said, snapping the case closed.

She nodded, feeling her eyes burn. She willed herself not to cry. She'd shed a million tears since the "lapses" in memory had begun, all wasted. Another million since the loss of her baby.

He touched her arm and she turned into him, stepping into his arms as naturally as if she'd done it dozens of times before. Maybe she had.

He held her, his arms strong and yet gentle around her. "We're going to find them," he breathed against her hair. "Find our baby if she's out there. And bring down those bastards. I promise."

The heat in his voice matched the warmth of his body. She leaned into his strength, soaking it in, telling herself she had to trust the instinct that had told her the father of her baby had been a good man.

And if it turned out her instincts were wrong about Slade Rawlins?

Chapter Eight

Her heart quickened as her body responded to being in his arms, the scent and feel of him teasing her memory. Taunting her with flashes of the two of them, naked as jaybirds, sweating and panting and—

She pulled back, stunned by the images. Even more stunned by the wanton desire she'd felt. But could she trust any of it? She looked at him, intensely aware just how dangerous this man could be if her instincts were wrong about him.

"I'm ready to go," she said, the break in her voice betraying her.

"Good," he said, but didn't move as he reached to thumb a tear from her cheek, the pad of his thumb rough against her skin, both comforting and disturbing.

His look told of an intimacy between them that frightened—and fascinated—her. Her heart drummed, her pulse a roar in her ears as his gaze moved slowly, deliberately to her lips.

He was going to kiss her! The thought sent a bolt of panic through her. Panic. And a stirring inside her that made her weak. She stared, hypnotized as his full, sensual mouth hovered only a breath over hers, afraid he would kiss her, afraid he wouldn't.

She waited, time suspended, her heart pounding as if to escape her chest. Would his kiss ignite that passion? Would it prove she was the woman he'd told her she'd been? The passionate, loving, blissfully satisfied woman she yearned to be? But mostly, would his kiss prove that he was telling her the truth, not only about him, but them?

Or would it only confirm that it had all been a lie, including a passion they had never shared.

His gaze rose again to her eyes and she knew. He wasn't going to kiss her. She felt a stab of disappointment and turned away, groping for her suitcase.

His hand brushed hers as he reached around her to take the case from her. She thought she felt a tremor course through him as they touched.

"Come on," he said, his voice as rough as his thumb had been. He dragged the suitcase from the bed and carried it into the living room.

Shaken and weak, her blood a dull thrum in her ears, she remembered her cosmetic case in the bathroom and went to get it, needing a few moments to herself.

When she came back out, he had the suitcase and the painting by the door. The broken glass was all cleared up.

The phone rang. Her gaze sprang to his. "Should I answer it?" she asked in a whisper, the apartment suddenly too quiet, the ringing too loud.

He seemed to hesitate. "Do you have caller ID?"

She nodded and stepped into the studio. "It's Inez."

"Wait." The phone rang again. "Do you have an extension?" he asked so close behind her he startled her.

"In the bedroom."

She let it ring once more, then picked up, watching

through the bedroom door as he did the same. "Hello?" Her voice sounded strange even to her.

"Holly?" Inez demanded in a tone that belied her years. "What's wrong?"

She wanted to laugh. Everything was wrong. Inez, of all people, should know that. But Inez put anything unpleasant from her mind, ordering the world to be the way she wanted it, come hell or high water.

That rankled Holly and shocked her. She usually had more patience with Inez. And yet part of her wondered why it hadn't rankled long before now.

"What could be wrong?" she asked unable to hide the sarcasm, which, of course, was wasted on Inez.

"You sound...strange."

She felt strange.

Slade gave her a warning look.

"I must have dozed off," she improvised.

He nodded his approval.

"I was worried about you," Inez said. Holly heard the clear, sharp tap of the elderly woman's cane on stone. "I was concerned that you might have gone off on another one of your...escapades."

Escapades? Was she referring to the pregnancy? Or the loss of the baby? Or was the "escapade" the hiring of Slade Rawlins? She felt a hot coal of resentment burning deep in her as she looked over at Slade. Why had she put up with Inez's interference in her life for so long?

"I want to talk to you about the private detective you hired," Inez said.

"This really isn't a good time," Holly said.

Inez continued as if she hadn't heard. Or didn't care. "I know this last year has been hard on you, losing Allan, then the baby."

"The baby had nothing to do with Allan," she heard herself say. "Or you." She'd never talked to Inez like this and she heard the shock in the older woman's tone.

"I beg your pardon?"

"I'm sorry, I'm just tired," Holly said, backing off just as quickly, just as she'd always done. Only this time it had been a sudden fear that had stopped her. A fear that upsetting Inez was…dangerous. Where had that come from?

She met Slade's gaze. He was frowning, watching her intently.

"Of course you're tired," Inez agreed, sounding wary. "You're just distraught. You always are when you do something foolish. I have tried to weather these episodes with you, dear, but this last one…. I know you haven't been yourself and I try to make allowances for you. Obviously, dear Allan's death hit you much harder than even you want to admit. That really is when this all started."

No, Holly thought. It all started about the time she met Allan. And Inez.

"But hiring a private investigator," Inez was saying. "It's so…common and…seedy."

Holly started to speak but Inez cut her off.

"Let's not discuss it further. It will only upset you to realize you've had yet another one of those embarrassing and tragic lapses in judgment. You're blaming yourself for the death of that baby, and Lord knows the guilt over that unfortunate pregnancy had to have contributed to the stillbirth. How could it not? But hiring a detective…?"

Holly thought she'd scream if she heard another word. Her head ached and she felt sick to her stomach. "Hiring Slade Rawlins wasn't a mistake." She didn't sound convincing even to her own ears, and she didn't dare look at Slade.

"There is no need to try to justify it," Inez said. "We all have made mistakes. Certainly none as extraordinary as yours," she added with a sniff, "but still, just look at the decisions you've made since Allan's death. They speak for themselves. I know Dr. Parris discussed your guilt over Allan's death with you at the sanitarium."

Holly shot a look at Slade again, embarrassed. Inez seemed intent on reminding her of the sanitarium and her mental instability, but now she was insinuating that Holly was responsible for Allan's death. Hadn't Slade already questioned the same thing?

"Dr. Parris never said anything to me about my having guilt over Allan's death," she said defensively.

Silence. "I was there on several occasions during your sessions when he discussed this very thing with you, Holly. Are you telling me you don't...remember?"

Panic raced through her, making her limbs weak with fear. She gripped the phone tighter, her hand trembling. That wasn't possible. She would have remembered. Or would she have?

Even more panicked, she suddenly realized that she couldn't remember *any* sessions with Dr. Parris when Inez had been there.

"Holly?" Inez asked. She sounded too cheerful as if she had Holly right where she wanted her. Scared. Unsure. Beaten back. Holly was shocked even to think it. Inez was her only family now.

A bubble of hope floated up from inside her as a clear, strong thought surfaced: Dr. Parris had seen her during these blanks in her memory. A sense of relief swept over her. First Slade. And now Dr. Parris. Only, Dr. Parris was a trained psychiatrist. He could make sense of this.

"Holly, are you still there?"

"Yes," she finally managed to say. She couldn't wait to tell Slade about Dr. Parris, about her lack of memory of the sessions with Inez and what it might mean.

"I had just forgotten those sessions with you and Dr. Parris," she lied, not sure why.

Inez was silent for a moment. "You mustn't castigate yourself. Once you're well... In the meantime, I've taken care of it. I'll have my lawyer pay off that private detective so he won't be bothering you anymore and I've spoken with Dr. O'Brien. He agrees rest is probably the best thing for you now especially since—"

"Dr. O'Brien?"

"Yes, he feels he can be much more beneficial to you than Dr. Parris. You need help, Holly, and please don't argue—"

"I think you're right," Holly interrupted.

"You do?!"

Even from this distance she could see the tightening of the muscles in Slade's jaw, the hard anger in his gaze and his manner. He, too, seemed to be clutching the phone.

"Yes," Holly said, suddenly feeling better. Her head still ached and her stomach was still upset, but her mind felt clearer than it had in a long time.

"Well, that's good that you agree." Inez sounded off balance, even a little disappointed, as if she'd expected a fight and had been ready for it. "You don't even have to recommit yourself since your old com-

mitment papers are still in force. I think you should
return to Evergreen at once. For your own good. Dr.
O'Brien said he would make arrangements to have you
picked up tonight.''

Slade was shaking his head.

"I'm really too tired tonight," Holly said.

"That's exactly why you need to—''

"Why don't I call you in the morning?" Holly said,
getting a nod from Slade. "I just want to go to bed
now."

"You're sure?" Inez said, an edge to her voice. She
wasn't pleased. "You *are* taking your pills, aren't
you?"

"Yes," she said, shooting a glanced at Slade. He
had that hard angry expression on his face again. Was
he right about the pills?

"They've made me very drowsy for some reason,"
she said. She softened her tone. "I really do appreciate
your concern, and I think you're right about me needing help."

Inez seemed hesitant to hang up as if not convinced.
"Well, then, get a good night's sleep. I'll talk to you
first thing in the morning."

"Yes, I'll do that." She hung up, feeling worn out
by the encounter with her sister-in-law, and she realized it was always like this. So much easier to give in
to Inez than to fight her. Just as it had been with Allan.

Only this time, she hadn't given in. The thought
buoyed her spirits.

"No wonder you think someone has been manipulating you," Slade said as he came into the living
room. "But what the hell was that about recommitting
yourself?"

"I agreed I needed help—not recommitting. I remembered something," she said excitedly. "When Inez was talking about Dr. Parris and Evergreen I realized I couldn't recall *any* discussions I had with him while Inez was there."

Slade lifted a brow. "That's a memory?"

"Don't you see, I must have been in one of my...blanks. But that means Dr. Parris would have observed this. He might know what was wrong with me based on the way I was acting." She saw Slade's expression. "I know what you're thinking. That I have some sort of personality disorder." It certainly sounded as though that was the case to her.

"You don't have a split personality," he said, sounding more convinced than she had expected. "I don't know much about personality disorders, I'll admit. And you're different from the Holly Barrows I knew this time last year. But not *that* much different. In fact, you seem to be becoming more and more like her all the time. With the kind of stress you've been under, I think it would be just the opposite. Once all your memory returns—" He broke off and shrugged, his gaze gliding over her face as gentle and warm as a caress.

She felt a rush of gratitude. Whether he was right or not, he was trying to reassure her and she appreciated that more than he could know.

And she did feel...different. Stronger. Just standing up to Inez— "Dr. Parris should be able to help us," she said again, hoping it were true.

He smiled at her, making her wonder if he thought her naive. "Maybe he does have some answers," he agreed, perhaps a little too easily. "Or this Dr. O'Brien your sister-in-law was so anxious for you to see might have."

She watched him walk to the door and pick up her suitcase and the painting, his words echoing in her ears.

"Let's get out of here." He seemed even more anxious to get away from her apartment now. Because of Inez's call? Was he worried Inez and Dr. O'Brien wouldn't wait until morning to come get her?

She realized why Slade had wanted her to take the call. He suspected Inez was somehow involved. And now, it seemed, he was even more suspicious.

Holly quickly followed after him, not so sure he wasn't right. Just before he turned out the light, the glare caught on her painting, highlighting the monsters huddled at the end of the bed. She had a flash of realization so strong it stunned her. Not a memory. But a feeling. Almost a warning. Something *had* been controlling her life. Something much more malevolent than Inez Wellington.

But the question was: Was it still in control?

Chapter Nine

Slade stepped out into the night, Holly right behind him. The top of the stairs were dark, the sky overhead a deep cold midnight blue, the December air frosty and wet with the promise of snow. Slade descended the steps, the day-old snow crunchy under his feet. He stopped at the bottom of the stairs to search the street, knowing that what he feared most wasn't waiting for them in the dark.

He took Holly's hand as they crossed the street to his pickup. He shivered, but he knew it wasn't from the cold. He was scared as hell.

Once behind the wheel, he started the truck and pulled away, watching in his rearview mirror.

"You're scaring me," she whispered, turning to look back.

"Sorry," he said. "Just force of habit."

But he couldn't help checking his rearview mirror as they left Pinedale, couldn't help feeling as though something was after them, because deep inside he believed something was.

No car lights flashed on behind them. But then he didn't think Dr. O'Brien had had time to round up a couple of orderlies and a straitjacket and drive to Pinedale. There was no doubt in Slade's mind though, that the doctor was on his way.

Nor did he think they were being followed. At least not in the usual way. What was after them was too hi-tech to use something as primitive as a tail.

Pinedale seemed hunkered down for the night as he drove through the deserted streets. After all, it was cold and late and Christmas Day.

Hard as it was to admit, he knew the fear he felt had nothing to do with Dr. O'Brien, Inez or even monsters dressed like Halloween ghouls. It was the fear he was in over his head. That Holly didn't need a private investigator. That she needed a shrink. That he was dead wrong and that, by getting her hopes up, he was only going to make things worse.

But he'd heard Inez on the phone. He had the pills in his pocket. Even if the pills didn't prove what he suspected they would, any fool could see that Holly was in trouble.

Selfishly he wanted the Holly he'd known—and who'd known him—back. And he wanted their baby. If Holly's memory of the little girl with dimples was real.

Unfortunately, he was smart enough to know that once whoever was behind this found out Holly was starting to remember, they might decide to get rid of the evidence. And that had him running scared.

He couldn't wait to get to Shelley's and build a fire. He needed the warmth of his sister's house tonight. A hard cold block of ice had settled inside him. He'd never felt so cold.

But he had one stop he had to make first. He glanced over at Holly. She sat huddled against the door staring out at the darkness, her face pale in the glow of the dash lights. He wondered what it must be like, having huge chunks of time you couldn't account for. Doing things that you wouldn't normally do. And waking up not knowing what you'd done. Or why.

The worst of it was, he didn't want to believe what was staring him dead in the face. He was one of those missing chunks of time. He wasn't sure who or what had kept him hidden inside her. And that had him worried. He hoped it would be as simple as the bottle of prescription drugs now snug in his pocket. But he doubted he could get that lucky.

"WHY ARE WE HERE?" Holly asked, unable to hide her sudden irrational fear, as he pulled into the hospital parking lot.

He glanced over at her in surprise. "Sorry, I should have told you. I want to find out if anyone has heard from the admitting nurse who was on duty Halloween night."

"Carolyn Gray." Holly had a bad feeling about the nurse. One she couldn't shake. "Do you think—" She hated to even voice her fear. "—that they would actually…kill someone to keep them quiet about this?"

"They stole our child, Holly. That's kidnapping, a federal offense. But still a step down from murder." He seemed to be studying her. "Are you afraid to go in the hospital? Because of the commitment papers?"

She shook her head. "Just bad memories." She'd been fine earlier in the day when they'd come here. She couldn't explain what had her scared now. She'd never been afraid of the dark. Or hospitals. Or monsters. But she was now.

"Don't worry," he said, his voice as soft as his gaze in the semi-darkness of the pickup cab. "I won't let them take you back to the Institute. No matter what I have to do.''

Impulsively she reached over to give his gloved hand lying on the seat between them a gentle squeeze. ''Thank you. For everything.''

''Thank me when this is all over,'' he said, looking uncomfortable. ''I haven't done much to protect you so far.''

They found the head nurse in the break room, sitting at one of a half-dozen round tables, reading. Mrs. Lander, according to her name tag, was a small woman dressed in an immaculate white uniform. Just the way she was sitting, her back ramrod straight and a no-nonsense aura about her, told Holly she would not be easy to work for.

''Yes?'' Mrs. Lander enquired, as she looked up from her reading.

Slade showed her his identification. ''Carolyn Gray is a key witness in a case I'm involved in. Have you heard from her?''

''Yes,'' Mrs. Lander said, a great deal of disapproval in that one word. ''She called yesterday to say she had taken another job and wouldn't be coming back.''

The same day Holly and Slade had gone to Carolyn's apartment to find it hastily cleaned out.

''You spoke to her yourself?'' he asked.

''No, the receptionist took a message.''

''But the receptionist was sure it was Carolyn Gray?'' he persisted.

Mrs. Lander looked from Slade to Holly. ''The receptionist is new, but the woman called herself Carolyn Gray. Why would she lie?''

Holly wandered over to a bulletin board full of photos, afraid Carolyn Gray might have had an accident like the midwife, Maria Perez.

"You don't seem surprised Carolyn Gray would leave without giving proper notice," Slade was saying.

"No."

"Why is that?"

"Why the interest, Mr. Rawlins?"

"I think she might be in trouble."

"I think with Carolyn that goes without saying," the nurse retorted. "Carolyn didn't take her job seriously. There were times she would leave her post without telling anyone. We often had a hard time finding her when we needed her."

Interesting. Holly moved along the bulletin board, wondering if Carolyn Gray was one of the nurses in the candid snapshots tacked up there. The snapshots made the hospital look like a fun place to work.

"What do you think the problem was?" Slade asked.

"Men. She liked men, especially doctors. I caught her once coming out of an empty room with one of the doctors."

"Which doctor?" he asked.

"I really can't say." Holly heard the scrape of a chair and turned to see the nurse on her feet. She closed the book she'd been reading. "I really need to get back to work."

"Can you tell us what Carolyn Gray looks like?" Holly asked. "Maybe there's a photo of her over here?" She motioned to the bulletin board.

The nurse seemed to hesitate, but walked over to the snapshots. She lifted several that had been tacked over older ones. "This one wouldn't help you. She's wearing a costume."

Holly felt her heart leap in her chest. "May I see it?"

The nurse removed the photo and handed it to her. "It was taken during the Halloween party."

Holly almost dropped the photograph. In between two other people dressed as monsters was the exact costumed monster Holly had painted.

"Which one is Carolyn?" she managed to ask, surprised her voice didn't betray her.

Nurse Lander pointed to the monster in the middle— the one from Holly's painting. "That's Carolyn. For what it's worth."

It was worth a lot. Holly handed the photo to Slade. He looked as taken aback as she was.

The nurse rummaged through the other snapshots on the board, grumbling about what a mess the bulletin board was. "Here's one of Carolyn. It's a fair likeness."

Holly took the photo the nurse handed her. It was of a women in a nurse's uniform standing behind the admitting desk. Carolyn Gray was a buxom woman, tall and broad-shouldered. In her costume, Holly could have mistaken her for a man.

She handed the photo to Slade.

"Why monsters?" he asked.

"Actually, I think it was Carolyn's idea," Nurse Lander said. "She was in charge of the party. She *made* her costume, which goes to show she has some talent— at least for the hideous. I think she won Most Frightening for it."

Holly could believe that. She searched the rest of the photos from the party on the bulletin board for the other two monsters, but unlike Carolyn's costume, the rest were pretty uninspired—and none of them familiar.

"Do you mind if we take these two with us?" Slade asked Lander. "I'd be happy to return them."

The nurse shook her head. "They're all yours," she said with a wave of her hand. She glanced at her watch. "If there is nothing else—"

"Just one thing, Carolyn would have had a check coming so I'm sure she gave you a forwarding address when she called, or at least her new place of work, so you could send it. If she really was the person who called."

The nurse pursed her lips. "She asked that her check be sent to Evergreen Institute. That's all I can tell you." Mrs. Lander swept past him and out the door.

"Sweet heaven," he breathed, after the nurse left, his gaze coming to Holly.

She nodded, still shaking. "Carolyn Gray was one of the monsters and now she's working at Evergreen."

"Do you recognize any of the other masks?" he asked.

She shook her head. The photos had been taken at random and probably not everyone had ended up on the bulletin board—even if they'd all been photographed. Or maybe all the monsters hadn't been part of the hospital crew that night.

"Anyone dressed as a monster would have had the run of the hospital Halloween night," she said. "All they would have had to do was dress as monsters."

"My thought exactly. They could have brought you in and no one would have been the wiser."

"Except Carolyn. She was at the birth, Slade."

He nodded. "The always-disappearing-from-her-post Carolyn Gray. You had to have given birth close to the hospital then. Close enough that Carolyn could slip out and slip back in without causing too much notice.''

''And even if she did get noticed, everyone would just think she was meeting one of the doctors,'' Holly added. ''Too bad we don't know which doctor.''

ONE MONSTER DOWN, Slade thought as he drove to his sister's. Two to go.

All he needed now was to find out where Holly had given birth. He still didn't have squat for proof, but there was no doubt in his mind it was all true.

Carolyn Gray was working at Evergreen. Or at least having her check sent there.

He felt even more jumpy, more anxious, after seeing the photos at the hospital. Don't think there are no crocodiles just because the water is calm, his father used to say.

And the water was anything but calm.

He got out and opened the garage door, then drove inside and waited until the door closed solidly behind them before he felt safe.

''Holly?'' She hadn't moved. Hadn't said a word since they'd left the hospital. And now she sat staring blindly at the front wall of Shelley's garage as if... ''Holly?''

''I knew one of them,'' she whispered.

He didn't have to ask who she meant. The monsters.

''I remember thinking, 'My God, I recognize that voice.'''

Sweet heaven. ''A man's or a woman's voice?'' he asked quietly.

She shook her head slowly. ''I just remember feeling disbelief. Like, how can this be? Not this person?'' She glanced over at him. "Someone I know took our baby. Someone I...trusted."

Like a doctor, he thought.

As he got out of the truck and led Holly into Shelley's house, he realized that this monster she'd recognized might also be someone *he* knew.

He got Holly settled in the spare bedroom, then went downstairs to scare up some dinner. He'd just put one of Shelley's casseroles in the microwave to defrost, when the phone rang. For just a moment, he thought it might be Inez. But Inez couldn't have found him that quickly.

He and Shelley didn't share the same last name. Shelley had been married for a very short time. Her husband had been killed in a motorcycle accident. She'd kept his last name, Baxter.

"Hello?"

Silence.

"Hello?" He felt the hair rise on the back of his neck. His heart pounded even though he told himself there was nothing to fear about a wrong number. Right.

The person at the other end of the line hung up. He stood holding the phone, trying to rationalize his sudden fear. It could have been anyone. It even could have been a real wrong number. Or a bad connection at the other end. It could have been Shelley calling from Tobago.

He started to put the phone down, but changed his mind. He dialed Chief L. T. Curtis, uncomfortable with the way he and the chief had left it earlier and needing someone sane to talk to. That is, if Curtis was still talking to him.

"What do you know about Evergreen Institute?" he

asked when Curtis answered, keeping things pretty much as they'd been for years.

If the chief was surprised to hear from him, it didn't show in his voice. "You finally decided to see a shrink?" the cop asked. "Probably not such a bad idea."

The defrost timer went off on the microwave. "I'm serious," Slade said as he hit the Reheat button.

"You're always serious. Do you have any understanding of the word *holiday?*" Curtis asked with a sigh.

"Not really," Slade said, realizing how true that was. "My client spent some time at Evergreen Institute."

"The case involving the alleged switched babies?"

"Yeah. What do you know about the place?"

"Why don't you ask your client?" the chief said. "Her late husband started Evergreen Institute."

"Dr. Allan Wellington?" He couldn't have been more surprised. Why hadn't Holly mentioned that to him?

"We're talking about the same place, right? That place that looks like a fortress off the old road to Butte?" Fenced and gated. Like the condos where Inez lived.

"The place with the stone spires sticking up out of the pines," Curtis said. "It was once a high-dollar private residence, built by some out-of-stater with more money than good sense—or taste. Dr. Allan Wellington bought it and started the first infertility clinic of its kind in this part of Montana."

Dr. Allan Wellington. Everywhere Slade turned, he kept running into the doctor. He didn't believe it was a coincidence. And to make matters worse, Curtis even sounded in awe of the good doctor. Sweet heaven.

"It's not an infertility clinic anymore, right?"

"No, it's a funny farm. More like a mountain resort than Warm Springs though," Curtis said. Warm Springs was where the state mental hospital was located.

"What about a Dr. Parris? Or a Dr. O'Brien?"

"Why the sudden interest in Evergreen?" the chief asked. "What does it have to do with your baby-switching case?"

"Maybe nothing," Slade said truthfully. He didn't want to talk about the case. Not yet. "Anything new on my mother?"

"No," Curtis said too quickly.

Not that he thought the chief would tell him until it was official anyway.

He tried to think of something else to say. "Happy New Year" just didn't quite cut it. "Well, thanks." He replaced the receiver, suddenly tired, mentally shot.

He wondered if there *was* something new on his mother's case. He knew the chief's threat was a good one and the last thing he wanted to do was lose his P.I. license. He'd have to be very careful when he started looking for his mother's lover again.

But right now all he could think about was Holly and their baby. First thing in the morning they'd drive up to Evergreen and see Dr. Parris. No, first thing, Slade thought, he'd have Holly's pills checked out by a pharmacist to see exactly what they were—and what they were capable of doing to her.

He didn't relish the idea of going to Evergreen to see Dr. Parris. He was scared about what the doctor would tell him about Holly. But what really had him worried was that Parris or O'Brien might try to recommit Holly. And Slade wasn't about to let that happen.

The phone rang, making him jump.

"I had some spare time, so I dug out the blood typing the lab did on Holly Barrows and her baby," a woman said, keeping her voice down as if she didn't want anyone to hear her. "I'm not supposed to do this but you seemed so worried...."

It took him a moment to realize it was the hospital admitting nurse he and Holly had met earlier. "What did you find out?" he asked, his heart in his throat.

"Mother and baby aren't related."

Slade felt his legs give under him. He sat down heavily at the breakfast bar, closed his eyes and took a deep breath. "You're sure?"

"Well, it's not as accurate as DNA testing, but hey, it's what they used to use before all these fancy-pants tests. You see, the way it works is this. If the mother has— Look, just trust me. The baby isn't hers. I've got to go. You did *not* hear this from me. When you pick up the report tomorrow, act surprised."

"One more question. Were there any other births on Halloween?" He could hear her rustling papers. "That's odd. No other births."

"Thank you. You didn't happen to call earlier, did you?"

"No," she said. "This was the first chance I got."

He hung up, shaken to the soles of his boots. The stillborn male infant wasn't Holly's. Wasn't theirs. Their baby could be alive! And now, he had enough evidence to get a court order to open the casket if it came to that.

He took a couple more deep breaths, just trying to deal with the fact that the baby buried in the Wellington family plot wasn't his. He felt weak with relief, weak with fear.

Knowing didn't help them find their baby. It just proved Holly had been right.

He turned at the sound of footsteps behind him. Holly appeared in the kitchen doorway, her wild mane of dark hair pulled back into a ponytail, her face looking freshly washed and shiny clean sans any makeup.

He felt as if struck by lightning. For just a moment he let himself hope— But when his gaze locked with hers, he could see that there was still no recognition of what had been between them. No memory.

He tried to hide his disappointment. "Dinner's almost ready," he said brightly. "I hope you're hungry."

She nodded, looking uncomfortable. "I heard the phone."

He tried to think of a way to tell her without just blurting it out. "The hospital called. One of the nurses decided to check the blood typing for us."

She paled, one hand reaching out to grip the counter top.

"The baby wasn't yours."

Her face relaxed in a swell of relief, her eyes filling. "I was right."

He nodded, desperately wanting to hold her and comfort her in some way. While it was a relief to know that the stillborn baby hadn't been theirs, it was almost more frightening not to know what had happened to their baby.

"Our baby is alive," she whispered. He prayed she was right. "Dr. Parris will help me get my memory back. I know at least one of the monsters. Once we find him…"

Or Carolyn, Slade thought. *If* Dr. Parris could get

Holly's memory back. *If* they could find the monsters. *If* the monsters knew what happened to the baby. Way too many ifs, Slade thought miserably.

The timer went off on the microwave. "Let's try to eat something now and not talk about it." He knew she probably wasn't any more hungry than he was, but they both had to eat. He turned to pull the casserole out, burning his fingers. Grabbing up two potholders, he took the casserole to the table.

She didn't argue. "I like your sister's house," she said, as if trying to make conversation, as she wandered around Shelley's kitchen. "Where do you live?"

"In an apartment next to my office. It's pretty basic." The truth was he wasn't much of a nester. He liked his sparsely furnished apartment just fine, no matter what Chief Curtis had said. Or Shelley. "I think you have a fear of domesticity," the chief had said the first time he'd seen the place. "Either that or no taste."

"It's fear of commitment," Shelley had said.

"I happen to like simplicity," Slade had argued. "If I want homey, I can always go to Shelley's."

Curtis and Shelley had looked at each other knowingly. "It's fear," they'd both said in unison.

Holly leaned against the breakfast counter. "Where did we…"

"Make love? Here. At my place. And a variety of other places—in and outdoors."

Holly seemed shocked by that information. "Outdoors this time of the year?"

"You didn't know you had it in you?" Obviously not.

She blushed and looked away, and he could have bitten his tongue.

"I just can't imagine—"

But he'd seen the answer in her eyes. She *had* imagined. Imagined the two of them.

She turned away as if to inspect Shelley's cookie-cutter collection on the kitchen wall. His mother and sister had been collectors. Maybe that's why Slade didn't collect. At least not "things."

Her hair was still wet from a shower. As he moved back into the kitchen, he picked up the scent of her. She smelled like spring, fresh and new as the first bright blades of green grass. He felt starved for—an end to the winter that had only just begun—and her.

As she started to step past him toward the table, he caught her arm. She stopped, motionless. He turned her slowly to him, her blue eyes as clear and deep as a mountain lake.

She wore jeans and a T-shirt. Both accentuated a full, rounded body he knew intimately.

The kiss was inevitable. He needed her in his arms, needed to hold her and feel her warmth, needed that reassurance that they would somehow get through this. Together. No matter what happened. He needed that more than his next breath.

He lost himself in her eyes, in all that blue as if untethered from earth and suddenly airborne. Her lips parted, the tiniest of sighs escaping.

His mouth lowered slowly, achingly to hers. A light brush. Their eyes locked as his lips again hovered over hers.

Her breath quickened, her heart answering the feverish beat of his own as he pulled her closer. He grazed her mouth again, heard her intake of breath, then her lips parted, opening to him. He dropped his mouth over hers, losing himself in the familiar touch and taste of her, finding in her the sanctuary he so desperately needed right now.

But he knew the kiss was more than finding sanctuary. It could possibly bring him back the woman he loved.

He was startled when she suddenly pulled away, her palms on his chest as she pushed back from him.

He looked down at her in surprise. Her face flamed and she lowered her lashes as if embarrassed. He cursed himself, backing up against the kitchen counter. She looked shaken, her cheeks flushed, her hands trembling.

"I'm sorry," he said, silently cursing himself again. "I told myself I wouldn't do that."

She shook her head, biting at her lower lip.

"You don't remember me, let alone us," he said in a rush. "You hired me to find out about the baby, not—" He slashed the air with his hand. "I'm sorry."

"It wasn't your fault. I wanted—" She looked away. "I was hoping the kiss would make me remember—"

Obviously it hadn't. "I guess I was hoping that, too." Hoping they could find comfort in each other's arms. He wouldn't admit it to her, but he was afraid, afraid that no matter what they did it would be too late for their baby.

"We should eat," he said.

She nodded and he moved aside to let her go to the table.

They ate, picking at their food, trying to make small talk, the kiss between them.

"You didn't mention that Dr. Allan Wellington started Evergreen Institute."

She looked up from her plate. "I just assumed you knew. Is it a problem?"

He shook his head. Dr. Allan Wellington was a thorn in his side that just kept needling at him.

She insisted on helping clean up the dishes. He caught her yawning and could see how drained she was.

"Go on up to bed. I can finish this."

She glanced toward the stairs.

"Don't worry, I'll be right down the hall if you need me. You're safe. Get a good night's sleep. Tomorrow we'll go see Dr. Parris. That is, if you want me to go with you?"

"Oh, yes," she said quickly. "Please."

He nodded, wanting to reassure her in some way, but feeling unable to. At least not with simple words. "Good night."

He watched her ascend the stairs, feeling anxious, antsy. He desperately needed to do something, something more than he had so far, something more than talk to a shrink.

She stopped part way up and turned to look back at him. "Thank you."

He had done so little, felt so confused, so frustrated. But at least he didn't have blank spaces in his life. Except for the last year when he hadn't been able to find her.

"Good night."

"Good night," he said again, knowing it would be anything but.

She disappeared up the stairs, him watching after her, longing in every cell of his body. He yearned for the Holly Barrows he'd known. For a moment during the kiss, he'd thought he'd felt the old Holly struggling to get out. But he could have imagined it, he'd wanted it so badly.

He swore, desperate to destroy whoever, whatever had done this to her. To them. Something or someone had brought her back into his life. Either her memory...or something dark and malignant could have sent her to him, setting them both up for a terrible fall.

What scared him was that if someone really had been controlling Holly, couldn't that person snatch her away again? Only this time, Holly might not be able to find her way back to him. This time, she might be as lost to him as their baby was to them at this moment.

With a chill, he thought of Inez's call and her insistence that Holly check herself back into Evergreen. Why had Inez been so adamant? Did she truly believe Holly was sick? Or did she know that Holly had begun to remember and was now a liability?

Slade stood in the kitchen, scared of his own thoughts. Did he really believe someone had...brainwashed Holly? He went into Shelley's office, booted up the computer and found the phone number on a Web page under Government Conspiracies.

He hadn't seen Charley Watts in years, not since Charley told him he thought the government was controlling Montana's weather. Slade didn't think the government was that organized.

Charley, a good twenty years older than Slade, had been the hippie janitor at the high school until—as locals called it—"Charley went off the deep end."

The deep end was government conspiracies.

But right now Charley was the only person Slade could think of to dare even mention the words *mind control* to.

"Hey!" Charley said when he answered. "Sure I remember you! What's going on?"

"What do you know about mind control?" Slade said, diving right in.

Charley laughed. "What don't I know? Hey, man, I've spent years researching it." He rattled off some code names. "What do you want to know?"

Slade was afraid he'd made a mistake calling Charley, but asked, "What are those?"

"Government research projects, man. You can't believe it."

No, Slade thought, he couldn't.

"We're talking using LSD on civilians to see if they would tell their darkest secrets, brainwashing with radiation, low frequency and ultrasonics, hypnosis—"

"Hypnosis?" Slade heard himself ask.

"Oh, yeah, man. Hypnosis and all kinds of drugs trying to come up with a hypnotic resistance to torture. They implanted secrets with special codes, turned regular men into killing machines and then erased their memories, man."

"They can erase memory? Give someone a drug, then hypnotize them and make them do things they normally wouldn't do, then erase their memory?"

"Dude, they can do a lot more than that!"

"But I always heard that a person wouldn't do anything under hypnosis that he wouldn't do under normal circumstances," Slade said.

"Yeah? Well, here's how it works," Charley said. "Say a guy who would never commit murder is drafted into a war. He'll kill on the battlefield, right? Well, with hypnosis, the mind becomes the battlefield. If we're told under hypnosis that it's a battlefield, then we believe it and will kill. It's all a matter of perception."

Slade frowned. Was it really possible? "But I

thought with hypnosis you went into an—'' He parroted the words he'd found in the dictionary. ''—altered state of focused awareness. I've always heard that you're awake, you know what's going on and you can stop it at any time.''

''You've been talking to shrinks, man,'' Charley said. ''If they can tell you you can't lift your damned arm during hypnosis, and, no kiddin', you try and you can't lift your arm, then why can't they make you do just about anything? It's all about mind control.''

''It sounds so…crazy.''

''Listen, governments have been doing this kind of research for years and lying about the outcome. They can program a guy to kill, they can get him to keep government secrets because he doesn't really 'know' anything on a conscious level—''

''Like the movie with Frank Sinatra, *The Manchurian Candidate?*'' Except that was fiction. Pure fiction, right?

''Kinda. Problem with hypnotically induced amnesia, there's memory leaks and that's how we've found out so much about what they've been doing. Guys are remembering.''

Slade gripped the phone. ''Memory leaks?''

''Bits and pieces of repressed stuff that suddenly pops up in dreams, flashbacks, you know…memories. So the government came up with screen memory. They fed 'em false stories to recall, like seeing spaceships and stuff like that, so no one will believe them.''

Slade shook his head, not sure how much of this he was buying. ''You mean the memories may not be real?''

''Not if the guy who programmed 'em did screen memories on 'em.''

Slade let out a sigh as he moved over to the kitchen window and looked out into the night. He felt exposed. He turned off the light. Something whipped by the window, startling him. Just snow blowing off the roof. He moved into the dark living room where the drapes were drawn.

"OK, let's say someone was programmed? How do you get them unprogrammed?"

"Could use hypnotic regression. Depends on how deeply the dude's been programmed. Sometimes just getting off the drugs and away from the programmer…"

"But if they get around the programmer?" Slade asked.

"Oh man, then they can be zapped into another state with just one word. There was this one case of this woman who got involved with this military man. She didn't even remember how they'd met. Missing-time experiences are common. So are personality changes."

Slade felt his heart begin to pound. It sounded too much like Holly. Too much like her experience with Allan Wellington. "Charley, you remember that place outside of town, Evergreen Institute?" He could hear Charley scrambling for a pen and paper. "I'm not saying anything is going on out there."

"Yeah, I got ya. I'll do some checking. I've got friends in low places." He laughed.

"Well, be careful. It could be dangerous," Slade said, realizing that that *was* something he did believe.

Charley let out a low whistle. "Man, not even Dry Creek is safe. Whoa, that blows me away."

"I don't have anything definite," Slade protested.

"No problem, man. If there's something to get, I'll get it."

Slade started to give Charley his phone number.

"Caller ID, man. There are no secrets anymore." Charley hung up.

Chapter Ten

December 26

A swollen gray sky spat snow as Slade and Holly drove through town early the next morning. With stores not yet open, the town felt abandoned.

Holly stared out the side window, watching the buildings sweep past, lost in thought. Last night when Slade had kissed her, she'd believed it would open up her memory like a floodgate. Instead, she'd felt confused and...afraid.

Now, she tried not to think about the kiss or Slade. All she could think about was the blood typing results in her purse. Inconclusive. The baby could have been hers.

So why did someone call from the hospital last night to say the blood typing proved the baby wasn't hers? She wanted to believe someone had "fixed" the results. But what was left of her rational mind knew that the young nurse who'd called Slade last night might not have understood the report.

She realized she was beginning to question her own sanity. What if they found out that she'd given birth somewhere near the hospital, alone? What if she'd been the person who'd brought the baby—and herself—to the hospital? Maybe there was no mystery at all. Just that she was very, very sick.

She tried to concentrate on what she would say to Dr. Parris. Thinking herself crazy wasn't helping. It was too close to what she suspected was the truth.

"Do you trust this Dr. Parris?" Slade had asked this morning at breakfast.

"Yes." The answer had come so quickly, she'd had to stop to think why. "He doesn't like Inez."

"He told you that?"

She recalled only one time Inez had come up to Evergreen. "There was a row," Holly told Slade. "I heard it from the sunroom. I didn't even know it was Inez, although I probably should have. I saw Dr. Parris rush by in the hall and I stuck my head out to see what was going on. That's when I saw Inez. She was giving the staff hell over something. I never did find out what. But Dr. Parris took her aside and spoke with her and she left, obviously angry. I caught the expression on his face before he saw me. He definitely didn't like her."

Now, as Holly stared out the side window at the passing town, she wondered what Inez had been so upset about. Inez hadn't stayed that time, but she must have come back if she'd sat in on sessions with Dr. Parris when he'd discussed Holly's possible guilt over Allan's death.

That seemed strange—that Dr. Parris would let Inez attend sessions, especially after their initial meeting. Or *had* that been the first time they'd met?

She rubbed her temples. Why could she remember Inez's first visit and not the others? Her head ached too much to think. She reached for her purse. *It's time for me to take my pill*. Her hand wavered just over her purse. Slade had taken the pills.

But that wasn't what stopped her. It was the thought: *It's time for me to take my pill*.

Where had that come from?

She felt a rush of panic as another thought rear-ended the first. *Take your pill. You need that pill. The pill is the only thing that helps you.*

But she *didn't* have to have the pills. She'd forgotten on Christmas Eve and hadn't taken one yesterday. It wasn't as if she was addicted to them. Suddenly she wasn't so sure about that. She definitely couldn't re-member feeling better after taking them. What she re-membered, though, was Inez insisting they helped.

She'd never been one to take pills. Not even aspirin. Except when she had a headache, which was rare. How had she come to depend on pills? Because since she'd met Allan and his sister, she'd seemed to have head-aches all the time.

No, she realized, that wasn't fair. The headaches had started before then. When her mother'd died. Holly'd had a headache the night she met Allan. Is that when he'd suggested the pills? Had it started that far back?

She shook her head, amazed that she'd been taking the pills for so long. Desperation. She realized she'd been desperate to believe *something* would help her memory loss, her mental confusion, her...fear that she was losing her mind. And she was still desperate, she reminded herself as she glanced over at Slade.

She noticed his hands and was fascinated by their size and shape and strength on the wheel. Long fingers. Strong, masculine hands. Hands that had touched her most private places. Shocked, she looked away.

Hadn't she just substituted him for the pills? Put her

faith in him, convincing herself that he would help her, just as she had the pills? Only she was clear enough now to know that he might not be any better for her than the drugs.

She closed her eyes for a moment. When she opened them, Slade was driving past the cemetery. Through the chain-link fence, past the towering stands of pine trees and the snow-cold tombstones, her eye caught the huge marble monument that was a memorial to Allan's and Inez's father. Next to it stood the god-like statue Inez had erected over Allan's grave and next to that—

Her heart leapt, and she sat up with a start. "Stop the truck!"

"What?"

"Go back to the cemetery. I saw someone. A woman. She was at the baby's grave." She didn't have to add at the bogus Allan Junior's grave.

Slade immediately swung the pickup around in a U-turn and sped back down the road to the cemetery turn-in. Through the pines, she could get only glimpses of the Wellington monument now. The hard-packed snow crunched under the truck's tires as Slade wound the pickup through the maze of narrow roads, turning at Holly's directions until she told him to stop.

The snowflakes grew larger, falling from the low, sullen clouds, silent as goose down. A magpie put up a ruckus in a nearby pine. The woman was gone.

"You're sure you saw someone?" he asked.

Without answering him, Holly opened her door, the cold morning air making her catch her breath. She pulled her coat around her as she walked toward the newest grave in the Wellington family plot. She hadn't been here since the funeral, not that she remembered much about that day. While it wasn't a complete blank, it felt surreal, just real enough to hurt.

"It could have been Inez you saw," Slade suggested as he joined her.

"It wasn't Inez," she said without looking at him. "There was no car." They both knew Inez couldn't have gotten away that quickly on foot. Whoever had been here had walked into the cemetery—not driven. As she neared the grave, she spotted the woman's footprints in the crusted snow near the grave. Beside an ostentatious sympathy spray was a tiny bouquet of blue silk forget-me-nots tied loosely with a blue ribbon.

"It was his mother," Holly said, knowing that to be true, the way she was starting to know herself again. She looked over at Slade. He was staring down at the tiny bouquet—and the footprints in the snow.

She followed his gaze as it chased the tracks through an empty part of the cemetery to the border of pines and the road on the other side.

Did the woman come here everyday? Or was this the first time? Would she be back? Holly felt her heart jump at the thought.

"It would be dangerous for her to visit the grave," she said, more to herself than to Slade. "That's why she came so early, why she parked over on the road and walked through the pines. She didn't want to be seen."

She turned to look at him then, blinking as if suddenly blinded by the sun. "If she knows that her baby was buried as my child—" A thought stopped her. Why would a woman agree to let her child be buried as someone else's? "Oh, my God!" Urgently she grabbed for Slade, getting a handful of his jacket in her fist. "She has our baby!"

SLADE FELT the hairs stand on the back of his neck as her words echoed through the frozen cemetery.

"She traded her stillborn for our child!" Holly cried. She jerked on his jacket as if she could physically convince him by shaking the truth into him. "Why else would she agree to this? Don't you see?"

He placed his gloved hand over hers and gently pried her fingers open, freeing his jacket to hold her hand in both of his. Her eyes shone too brightly. She tried to pull her hand away as if too nervous to hold still. He turned her palm up, sandwiching it between his hands as if to warm it, when the truth was he didn't want to let go of her, afraid she'd fly off in a dozen different directions in a thousand different pieces.

"Holly," he said quietly, hoping to stop her before she let her hopes run so high he couldn't get them back down without doing permanent damage. "Why would these...people go to that kind of trouble simply to replace this woman's child?"

She stopped, the light dimming a little in her eyes. "Maybe she's someone. She has a lot of money or—"

"Not by the looks of the flowers she brought," he broke in, hating to disappoint her.

"She just didn't want anyone to know she'd been here," Holly said.

"Then a spray like the one already on the grave would have been less conspicuous, don't you think? Or none at all."

He watched Holly's breath come out in frosty white puffs. Tiny specks of snow floated down to land in her dark hair, to catch on her lashes. She frowned, fighting what he was saying.

"Another thing," he said, motioning to the footprints in the snow. "Look at what she was wearing.

An old pair of sneakers, the tread nearly gone on the heels. The snow is deep on the way in from the road. Her feet had to be cold. Why didn't she wear snow-boots? Unless she didn't have any.''

''Maybe she was in too much of a hurry,'' Holly said. ''Or was too upset.''

He shrugged, giving her that.

Holly pulled her hand free of his, but didn't move away from him. He watched her blink, the tears making all that blue seem endless. ''If she doesn't have our baby, then she has to know who does, right?''

He couldn't take that away, too. ''I would think she'd have to know at least one of the players.'' He didn't want to tell her that the woman might have just been paid to give up her baby. Especially if she'd known just before the birth that the baby would be stillborn. But that would mean that some local doctor was in on the switch. How else could the people behind this have found her—and made some deal for her baby?

''She knows where her baby is buried,'' Holly said. ''She has to know about me.''

Maybe. If she really was the mother. The county was small. Dry Creek even smaller. All the woman had to do was check the obits in the paper to find her baby. He didn't believe this woman would know much. Just as he didn't believe she had their baby.

He took Holly's arm and turned her away from the grave, away from the towering Wellington monuments to the dead and back toward his pickup, managing to step squarely on Allan Wellington's grave in the process. It was a childish show of disrespect. He didn't like Allan Wellington. Nor could he entirely justify his animosity towards a dead man. But he planned to be able to soon. He fervently believed Allan was somehow involved in all this—even though the man had been dead for months. Slade felt it as surely as the winter cold around him.

"How do we find her?" Holly asked when they'd reached the pickup.

He'd already been thinking about that. The other mother, if that's really who she'd been, could be added proof that the babies had been switched. Plus that mother would have given birth at the same place Holly had. She might be able to help them with that as well.

"I'm not sure," he said as he climbed behind the wheel. He didn't have a clue how to find her. She wouldn't have gone for medical help even if she'd needed it. Too many questions would have been asked.

"You know, something's been bothering me," he said. "If these...monsters who delivered your baby, if they were doctors, why didn't they do an episiotomy? Why were you suffering from hypothermia when you arrived at the hospital?"

"Maybe they wanted it to look as if I'd given birth alone, without any help," she suggested as he started the truck.

"Maybe." He thought about her memory of the three ghouls appearing frantic, the feeling that something was wrong. "That seems a little too cruel, even for monsters. Maybe they didn't know what they were doing because they lacked the medical expertise. Maybe they weren't doctors at all." He didn't like that theory because it opened up too many possibilities. "Have you remembered anything more about the room? It wasn't just a bedroom in some house?"

She shook her head as she squinted out at the

gloomy day. ''The bed made me think it was a hospital because of the rails.''

Hospital-type beds could be rented. Or purchased.

''I don't know,'' she said with a sigh. ''I can't be positive it wasn't just a bedroom but— Wait a minute. The ceiling.'' Her voice had dropped to a whisper.

He looked over at her.

Her eyes were closed. ''The ceiling seemed too high for a regular house. And…there was something on it.''

He waited, afraid to speak for fear of making the memory—if that's what it was—slip away.

''A mark.'' She opened her eyes and frowned.

''You mean like the roof leaked?'' he asked when she didn't continue. ''Or the plaster cracked?''

She nodded. ''It was in the shape of something large and scaly.''

He stared at her for a moment, then looked back to his driving. ''Like a dragon?''

''Or some kind of monster,'' she said with a sigh. ''Obviously, I saw monsters everywhere I looked,'' she added, her tone dismissing the ceiling design and the memory as useless.

He wanted to assure her that every possible memory was important. But three monsters at the end of the bed and another on the ceiling?

He shifted down at the edge of town, the pills he'd taken from her rattling softly in his coat pocket. Who knew what those pills could have made her see? he thought as he pulled into the drugstore parking lot, anxious to find out.

''Do you mind if I wait here?'' she asked.

He would much rather have had her with him, but the pharmacy was near the front of the store and he knew he would be able to keep her in sight. "I'll get you something for your headache."

"How did you know I had a headache?" she asked in obvious surprise.

He shrugged. "You get this little ridge between your brows when your head hurts," he said, feeling strangely shy about revealing the things he knew about her.

She studied him openly for a moment. "You do know me, don't you?"

He nodded, his gaze brushing hers, sparking like flint on granite. He opened his door, breaking the connection, telling himself to let her take the time she needed, hoping she had the time to take.

Last night, unable to sleep, he'd stayed up going through old photo albums from when he and Shelley were kids. This morning he'd put in a call to her, just wanting to hear her voice. But she hadn't been in her room. He'd left a message asking her about the twin-angel Christmas ornament, asking her to call him. The moment he hung up, he wished he hadn't said anything about the ornament. He hadn't meant to.

He felt disconnected, dreading what he might find out, knowing somewhere deep inside himself that the news on neither case would be good, and wondering how he would be able to tell Holly. And Shelley.

"Slade Rawlins?" Jerry Dunn said when he saw him. "I haven't seen you in a month of Sundays."

Jerry and Slade had gone to school together. They were two of a handful of classmates who still lived in Dry Creek. The difference was, Jerry had left long enough to become a pharmacist. Slade felt anchored here by the past.

He reached across the counter to shake Jerry's outstretched hand. For a pharmacist, Jerry had a hell of a grip. He'd played fullback on the football team and looked as if he still worked out. Jerry had married his high-school sweetheart and started a family. Slade knew why Jerry had stayed in Dry Creek. Jerry had inherited his father's drugstore and pharmacy when his father'd retired.

"So how's business?" Slade asked, although the drugstore was empty except for a young clerk at the front.

"Crazy before Christmas. Fortunately it's slowed down, but hey, flu season is coming." Jerry grinned. "It will pick up."

Slade pulled the container of pills from his pocket. "I need to know what these are."

"Sure." The former fullback took the bottle, checked the prescription, then shook a couple of the pills out into a small plastic tray. "Looks like a generic of Xanax. A common anxiety medication," he added when he saw that the name rang no bells for Slade.

"Strong?"

"Not really."

Slade glanced toward the truck and Holly. She'd leaned back against the seat, her eyes closed. He'd hoped Jerry was going to tell him that the pills were something strong enough to cause memory loss. But Slade knew it had been a long shot. What pill was strong enough to cause a woman to forget months out of her life?

"Is there any way to test these pills?" he asked. "A lab, somewhere I can take them?"

"What about the Butte hospital's computer?" the young clerk asked. "Can't they run the number on the pill?"

Slade hadn't heard her approach. She was young, college-age, blond and with a look of intelligence. Her name tag said she was Penny.

"I was just getting ready to suggest that," Jerry said, obviously not happy about the interruption. "Want me to call for you?" he said to Slade.

"I can do it," Penny said. "I've been going to pharmaceutical school and I need the practice," she told Slade. "Isn't that what you always tell me when it comes to your grunt work, Jerry?" She grinned as she picked up the phone, reaching over to take the tray and pills from Jerry.

"See this," she said to Slade as she waited for the hospital to answer. She pointed to a small indentation that appeared to be a letter and a number. "The hospital computer data base can tell you what generic it is."

"How long does it take?" he asked.

"Not long."

"Anything else you need?" Jerry asked, sounding a little testy.

"Yeah, something for a headache."

"I know what you mean," Jerry said, coming out from behind the counter to help him. While they moved through the drugstore, Slade kept an eye on Holly. Jerry asked about Shelley and made polite conversation. He and Jerry never had had much in common, Slade realized.

Armed with a bottle of painkillers for Holly's headache and a pop out of the cooler, he and Jerry returned to the pharmacy counter. The clerk was just getting off the phone.

"Wow," she said, eyeing one of the pills as she hung up the phone. "I don't think I've ever seen one of these. They're the same color, size and shape as Xanax, but they're Halcion.''

"Are you sure?" Jerry said in surprise.

"What's Halcion?" Slade asked.

Jerry let out a low whistle. "Halcion is an oldie, been around literally for years. It's a sedative hypnotic," he said, obviously stealing the young clerk's thunder.

Slade felt his breath rush from his lungs. "A hypnotic?"

"There was this big case in Utah," the clerk said enthusiastically. "A woman was taking Halcion and killed her mother. Got off too."

"Side effects?" Slade managed to ask.

"Oh yeah," she said before Jerry could. "Disorientation, light-headedness, mental confusion, loss of memory, paranoia."

He felt a little light-headed himself. "Addictive?"

"Highly," Penny said. "This stuff is dangerous. I can't imagine a pharmacist making a mistake like this." She eyed the prescription. "The bottle's so old it's hard to read where the prescription was first filled. Halcion isn't easy to come by. It's so dangerous that you can only get ten pills at a time."

Unless you knew someone who could get you the stuff without raising suspicion. The question was, who had put the Halcion in the Xanax bottle? Inez was the obvious choice.

Jerry picked up the bottle, frowning at the prescription. "Dr. Allan Wellington?"

"It's an old prescription."

"I guess. He's been a dead a while, hasn't he?"

Not long enough, it seemed.

"Holly Barrows?" Jerry said, still reading the prescription.

"A client of mine. Don't worry, I won't let her take any more of them."

"Good thinking. You want me to throw out the pills for you?"

"No," Slade said quickly. "I'd like to hang on to them for a while."

Jerry put the pills back in the container. "I'd throw them out if I were you."

Not likely. They were evidence.

Jerry glanced toward Slade's pickup and the woman sitting inside it, openly curious.

Slade wasn't interested in satisfying his curiosity. He thanked Jerry and his assistant for their help and paid for the headache pills and the soda. Behind Jerry on the wall was a family photograph of Jerry and his wife Patty and a couple of towheaded little boys about six and four.

Slade felt a tug at the sight of the kids and the happy family. He tried to imagine a photo of him and Holly and their little girl—and couldn't.

"You should see the latest photos of the kids," the clerk said, noting what he'd been staring at. "They are *the* cutest things."

He thanked Jerry and Penny again and left, the Halcion safe in his pocket.

GRATEFULLY, Holly took the bottle of tablets and the drink Slade handed her as he climbed into the pickup.

"Thanks."

He was right. She had a blinding headache. After she tried unsuccessfully to unscrew the cap on the pill bottle, he took it from her, opened it and shook two tablets into her outstretched palm.

She fumbled to pop the top on the soda can, downing both pills in a swallow of throat-tingling cold liquid. She closed her eyes for a moment, knowing why he'd gone into the pharmacy, afraid of what he'd found out.

"The pills?" she said after a moment.

"They're probably responsible not only for your headache, but also your memory loss," he said as he started the truck and pulled back out onto the highway.

"What are they?" she asked, shocked.

"They aren't what they say on the prescription."

That shouldn't have come as a surprise to her since Slade had already suspected as much. She listened while he told her about the hypnotic drug and its side effects.

She was too stunned to speak. "Then it was just the drug. Someone must have mixed up the prescription—"

"Not likely," Slade said. "I think there is more to this than just the drug. Did anyone besides Inez have access to the prescription?"

All she could do was stare at him. Inez. "You think she was the one who—?"

"It could depend on where she got the prescription filled."

Holly looked out the window at the passing town, remembering how Inez had asked last night if she'd taken her pill. How Inez had insisted she go back to Evergreen. How Inez had planned to fire Slade.

"The other day when I was at your sister-in-law's, someone buzzed at the gate," Slade said, not looking at her as he drove. "It was obvious Inez didn't want me to know who it was. But eventually, she answered the intercom. It was a Dr. O'Brien from Evergreen.''

Holly felt sick to her stomach. She had to fight back tears of anger—and pain. For the last year, Inez had been her only family. As difficult as Inez had been, Holly had trusted her.

"I feel like a fool."

"You shouldn't," Slade said. "The pills are identical to Xanax. You had no reason to believe they were anything but what they said they were on the bottle."

"Still…"

"I think your memory started coming back when you came to Dry Creek and forgot the pills in Pinedale," he said. "Maybe you did that on purpose."

Was it possible that on some subconscious level she'd suspected the pills weren't really helping her?

"I talked to a friend of mine last night," Slade was saying. "He said these kinds of drugs are used in conjunction with hypnosis."

Hypnosis?

"You said you felt as if someone was manipulating you," he reminded her. "Drugs and hypnosis have been used in mind-control experiments."

Hypnosis. She tried to grasp it, her thoughts scattering like bits of paper in the wind. She'd seen a hypnotist once in a bar in Butte. He'd made grown men hop around and cluck and flap their arms like chickens. No, not *like* chickens. The men had appeared to believe they *were* chickens.

"Did Dr. Parris use hypnotism on you at Evergreen?" Slade asked.

"I don't remember ever being hypnotized." She did remember, however, that a hypnotist, through hypnotic suggestion, could wipe out all recollection of a person ever being hypnotized. Case in point: the chicken/men at the bar. They'd gone back to their stools, confused by the laughter and applause, believing the hypnotist had failed to put big, strong men like them "under."

At the time, it had seemed silly. Now it was disturbing. "This drug I've been taking, would it make it easier for me to be hypnotized?"

Slade nodded, his gaze seeming to access how hard she was taking this. "I have a feeling you were also programmed to take the pills."

The words she'd heard in her head this morning echoed now. *It's time for me to take my pill.* Dear God. "So it is possible someone *has* been controlling me?"

"I'd say it's a whole hell of a lot more than possible."

Still, Holly hadn't really accepted the ramifications. Inez had given her the pills. Inez thrived on control. But Allan had written the original prescription. And when she'd met Allan, that's when it had all begun.

"But why? It has to be more than just the baby," she said, watching the dense snowcapped pines blur by as the pickup snaked up the narrow old two-lane road toward the summit of the pass—and Evergreen Institute. She hadn't seen another car for miles and had forgotten how isolated it was out here. "My memory lapses go back a whole year," she pointed out.

"I wish I knew," Slade said. "Unless they'd had something planned for you that far back."

"You mean—" She glanced over at him. "You don't think they purposely got you and me together?"

"No. For what purpose?"

"The baby?" she said. "Like you said, that's all they appear to have gained."

He drove in silence for a moment. "How could they know we would have a baby together?"

She stared at him. "Because they know everything about us. Once they were in control of my mind...they could control you as well."

He smiled over at her. "They couldn't make me fall in love with you."

"Maybe they hadn't planned on that." Hadn't planned on her going back to him this Christmas Eve for help. Hadn't planned on the bond that had drawn her to him. She wanted desperately to believe that. To believe she and Slade had the upper hand. It gave her hope that they could find their baby and get her back. "Just as they hadn't planned on my memory coming back and me coming to you for help," she said, hoping he'd agree.

He looked over at her and smiled. "I'd like to think we're one step ahead of them."

His smile warmed her to her toes. "Thanks," she said, feeling almost shy. She was changing, wasn't she? She felt stronger. Just knowing that she wasn't losing her mind helped. That it had been the pills making her feel that way and that someone had been unconsciously forcing her to keep taking the pills. All of it made her angry—and more intent on foiling their plans.

A thought struck her. "No one knows I've quit taking the pills or how much of my memory is coming back." The thought pleased her immensely. "How long do you think we have before they know?"

Slade slowed the pickup, turned into a paved, pine-lined driveway, bringing the pickup to a stop before an ornate locked steel gate.

"That all depends on whether Dr. Parris is in on it," he said as he rolled down his window and reached out to buzz the intercom of the Evergreen Institute.

Chapter Eleven

Dr. Parris seemed genuinely pleased to see Holly. He came from one of the long hallways, his footsteps echoing through the massive stone foyer as he moved toward the reception desk, a tall man with graying hair and long arms and legs that appeared almost disjointed. He reminded Slade of a marionette.

"Holly," Parris said, greeting her with a smile. "How are you?"

"That's what I hope to talk to you about," she said. "I'm sorry I didn't call for an appointment."

Parris waved that off, then looked to Slade, his smile still firmly in place. On closer inspection, Slade could see that the doctor seemed disheveled. His pale-blue smock was stained from the leaky pen stuck in the breast pocket and his name tag was askew. He didn't look like a man who could control anything—certainly not Holly's mind.

"This is a...friend of mine," Holly said. "Slade Rawlins."

The doctor offered his hand. "Pleased to meet you," he said, sounding as if he meant it. "Rawlins? Why does that name sound so familiar?" he commented more to himself than to Slade. "Come on down to my office."

Slade and Holly followed him down a long, wide marble hallway. The place looked like a palace. Outside, Slade had glimpsed a horse barn, a covered pool and indoor tennis courts. He had seen no patients and hardly any staff. He figured it had something to do with that wonderful scent of food he kept picking up. Not school-cafeteria-type food. A gourmet lunch from the smell of it, served somewhere deep in all this luxury.

The doctor's office was large but filled. The huge desk had long disappeared beneath an avalanche of papers and books. He had begun to stack books on the floor around his desk like a wall.

Slade watched him close the door behind them, then rush to uncover two chairs for them. "I usually don't use my office for therapy sessions, as Holly knows," he said by way of explanation to Slade.

"I have been concerned about you," he said to Holly when they were all seated. "I heard about your recent loss. I'm so sorry."

Slade found himself listening to the doctor's words and watching Holly's reaction. If she'd been hypnotized, hadn't Charley said that a catchword or phrase could be used to control her? But to his relief Holly seemed to have no reaction to Dr. Parris or his words other than gratitude.

"Thank you," she said and looked over at Slade.

"That's partly why we're here," Slade said, introducing himself as a private investigator. The doctor seemed a little surprised but not overly. "Holly has been experiencing some memory loss. I'm looking into the missing parts for her."

Dr. Parris swung his gaze to her. "You mentioned that before when you were here."

"That's just it," Holly said. "When Inez told me about the sessions she sat in on with you and me where—"

"Inez?" Dr. Parris interrupted, frowning. "She never sat in on any sessions with the two of us."

Holly stared at the doctor. "Are you sure?"

"Holly," he said, concern in his voice, in his expression. "You and I never *had* any sessions with Inez in attendance."

Slade watched her let out a long breath before she looked over at him, relief in her gaze and something more. Anger and an even stronger determination.

Not wanting Parris to know just how important that information was, Slade jumped in, "Did you ever hypnotize Holly during any of her sessions with you?"

Parris frowned. "No."

"Or prescribe Xanax?"

The doctor shook his head, his frown deepening.

"How about Halcion?"

"Halcion?" Parris said, sounding shocked. "Of course not. That's a hypnotic. Very dangerous."

"So no doctor you know here at the Institute uses Halcion in conjunction with hypnosis?"

The doctor looked horrified. "Perhaps you should tell me what this is about."

Slade looked at Holly, unsure how much they wanted to confide in Dr. Parris. "Were you aware Holly was taking Halcion?"

The doctor shook his head. "Not while she was an inpatient here."

"How can you be so sure?" Holly asked.

"Because it would have shown up in your blood work," Parris said.

Slade rubbed his eyes. "What about a nurse named Carolyn Gray? I understand she just started to work here?"

Parris shook his head. "We have made no new hires."

Another dead end. But why did someone want Carolyn Gray's check to come here? "When was Holly released from the Institute?" he asked, remembering the commitment papers.

"I'm afraid she wasn't," Parris said. "It was a most unfortunate incident. We aren't used to losing patients around here."

Slade glanced at Holly. She looked as confused as he did. "What incident was that?"

"Holly leaving the way she did," the doctor said. He glanced at each of them and frowned. "She just took off one afternoon during a huge snowstorm."

"Christmas Eve," Holly said.

"Yes, that's right, Christmas Eve," Dr. Parris agreed and shook his head. "Fortunately, your sister-in-law called to say you were safe, and we didn't need to continue looking for you."

Slade felt his heart drop like a stone.

"Inez called you?" Holly said, her voice cracking. "When was that?"

"That afternoon just before we were going to start a full-scale search," the doctor said.

Inez had stopped the search. Because she didn't want Holly found in the state she was in? Or because Inez knew that Holly was with Slade—as per plan?

Slade raked a hand through his hair, fighting every instinct in him that told him to get the hell out of this place as fast as possible. When Holly had run in front of his pickup on Christmas Eve a year ago, convinced someone was trying to kill her, she'd been running from this place, it seemed. And at the same time, Inez Wellington was calling Evergreen Institute to say that Holly was safe.

"What exactly is it the Institute does?" Slade asked, surprised that his voice sounded calm, in control, when he was more convinced than ever that something had happened to Holly *here,* something that had frightened her and made her leave on Christmas Eve in a blizzard, something that had her believing that someone was trying to kill her. And Slade no longer believed it was all in her mind.

"What goes on here?" Dr. Parris parroted as if he thought everyone knew. "Well, originally Dr. Wellington opened it to continue his research in infertility. After his death, it became more of a medical retreat. We now specialize in the needs of today's clients."

Clients, not patients. People with money, Slade thought. It would take a lot of money to run a place like this.

"Our clients often need a quiet, out-of-the-way sanctuary where they can relax and work on health-related issues such as weight loss, better nutrition, stress management, smoking cessation, insomnia, drug and alcohol addiction. These are stressful times wrought with social problems. Sometimes, as in Holly's case," the doctor smiled over at her, "our clients just need a place to rest."

It sounded so benign. "Kind of like a health club where you can decide if you want to work on your abs or your fear of heights."

Dr. Parris smiled as if relieved. "Exactly." No mind control here, his smile said.

"What about Inez Wellington?"

Parris looked confused.

"How is she involved with the Institute?"

"She isn't."

"Even when her brother ran the place?" Slade asked, not believing it.

"Not even then, that I was aware of," Parris said, seeming actually to believe it.

Slade didn't, not for a moment. Inez had some power either over the place or at least over one of the doctors—in particular Dr. O'Brien, the impatient man who'd been at her gate yesterday afternoon.

"Well, thank you for your help," Slade said, getting to his feet, relieved to be leaving.

"I'm not sure what help I've been, Mr. Rawlins," the doctor said as he got up to see them out. "Rawlins?" he said thoughtfully as he shook Slade's hand. "Marcella Rawlins?"

Slade felt himself tense. "She was my mother."

Dr. Parris nodded. "I thought so. A fine woman. I was so sorry to hear about…what happened. A terrible tragedy for everyone involved. I had wished there was something I could have done."

Slade stared at him. "Done?"

"For Lorraine. Obviously, there wasn't anything I could have done for your mother or Lorraine's son Roy at that point. But Lorraine…"

Lorraine Vogel. The mother of the young man who'd allegedly killed Slade's mother.

The doctor must have seen Slade's confusion. "I was afraid Lorraine wouldn't complete her training after everything that happened. She was training to be a nurse here at the Institute. But she did finish. Now she works part-time here—and part-time at the hospital.''

It took Slade a moment to find his voice. Lorraine worked at the Institute? And Slade's mother— ''You knew my mother?''

Dr. Parris seemed surprised by the question. ''Only to say hello in the hall really.''

''Here at the Institute?'' Slade asked.

Parris realized he'd made a mistake, but it was clear he didn't know how. ''Yes.''

''She was a patient here,'' Slade said.

Dr. Parris smiled and looked relieved. ''Yes.''

His mother was a patient here? How was it possible that he and his sister and his father hadn't known that? He couldn't remember even one day his mother hadn't been at the stove on his return from school or from playing in the neighborhood with friends.

''Back when Evergreen was a fertility clinic,'' Slade said, trying to put it together. ''Back when Dr. Allan Wellington was running the place.'' He felt something like a flash go off in his head and wondered if it was like this for Holly. A thought. A memory? A piece of knowledge just appearing in a bolt of crystal-clear bright thought. ''I was pretty young then, but, that's right, she came up here every Tuesday and Thursday.''

Dr. Parris beamed. ''That's right. She always had a kind word and a smile.''

Stunned, Slade was still trying to make sense of it. His mother had come up here every Tuesday and Thursday afternoon. No affair? But what had she come up here for? It couldn't have had to do with infertility—and his mother didn't drive. She'd been in a near-fatal car accident and had a deathly fear of driving.

Norma always drove her wherever she wanted to go. Or Slade's father, Joe.

Who had driven her to Evergreen twice a week? Not Joe, the person she'd said in her letter she didn't want to know about her afternoons away from home. So who had driven her? Not Norma. Dr. Wellington? Was he also the man who'd had Marcella Rawlins in his arms the day Norma had seen the two of them at the house?

Slade felt sick, all of it coming too close to home. "You have a very good memory, Dr. Parris. You probably remember that my mother didn't drive," Slade said as they moved out of the office and into the empty hall.

"Why, that's right," Parris exclaimed. "I think that's why she came up on Tuesdays and Thursdays, so she could ride with Lorraine on Tuesdays and Dr. Delaney on Thursdays. My, but that has been years ago. My memory serves me well."

Slade fought to breathe. Dr. Delaney?

"Give yourself some time," Parris was saying to Holly. "You're a strong young woman. You're going to be just fine."

"Thank you, doctor," she said.

"I didn't realize that Dr. Delaney worked here," Slade said, interrupting Holly.

"Only on special projects anymore. A fine man and a wonderfully compassionate doctor," Parris said. "Let me know if there is anything else you need. It is always nice to see you, Holly, and nice meeting you," he said again to Slade, then turned and disappeared back into his office.

Slade took Holly's arm as they started down the hall toward the exit. "Are you all right?"

"Yes. No. Inez lied about the sessions."

He nodded, wondering why Inez had done that. Unless it had been a test. A test to see if Holly was remembering.

"*And* she lied about where I was last Christmas Eve," Holly said, sounding angry and scared. "Unless she knew I was with you."

"Yes," Slade said. "I thought of that. Or maybe she just didn't want the staff up here looking for you. Any idea why you left here in such a hurry? You didn't even have a coat on when I found you."

She shook her head. "You said I thought someone was trying to kill me. Do you think it was just the pills?"

"Dr. Parris swears you weren't taking them while you were here," he pointed out. "Nor were you taking them when you were with me."

A door opened off to the right ahead of them. A woman in a business suit and heels came out carrying a large cinnamon bun and a mug of something hot. She headed down the hallway in front of them without looking back, her high heels clicking on the hardwood floor, turning off one of the many hallways.

Through the glass window in the office door, Slade spotted a desk and computer. Seeing no one else around, he quickly pushed the door open before it could shut completely. He pulled Holly into the office and closed the door behind them.

"What are you doing?" she whispered in obvious horror as he grabbed a straight-back chair from in front of the desk and stuck it under the door so it couldn't be opened from the outside.

"Buying time." He hurried around to sit down at the computer. "I want to see your file. And my mother's."

"Here, let me do that," she said after a moment of watching him try to call up files.

He moved to let her sit down and, standing behind her with his hands on the back of her chair, watched in awe as she quickly maneuvered her way through the system. "I didn't know you knew anything about computers."

She let out a quiet chuckle. "So, there is at least a little something about me that's still a mystery."

Her joking tone stirred old memories deep within him of the way it had been between them. "You will always be a mystery to me," he said softly.

She leaned back, waiting for the computer to respond, her scent filling him. Her hair brushed the tops of his hands, reminding him only too well of the feel of it against his bare skin.

He could see her reflection in the computer screen as her eyes came up to meet his. For the first time, he didn't see fear, but something just as familiar. A look that made him ache inside.

His hands slipped from the chair back to her shoulders. She pressed against the pressure of his fingers and closed her eyes. Slowly he moved his hands down her arms to her elbows as he bent over her, breathing her in, wanting to envelop her. She felt warm and solid, strong.

Her eyes opened and her gaze met his in the screen. Her lips parted, her look softening, deepening. He would have kissed her. The chance of getting caught be damned.

But just then the computer screen flashed. No Holly Barrows found.

He straightened, releasing her.

She typed in Holly Wellington. "Look at this," she

said. Under Medications, it read, None. "And this."
She pointed to a notation at the top of the file: Genesis
Project. When she clicked on it, the screen flashed:
Enter Security Code. She tried several. None of them
worked.

He heard the sound of high heels tapping down the
hallway. They grew louder as they approached. "See
if you can get Marcella Rawlins's file."

Holly typed in the name. "I can't find her. How long
ago was it?"

"More than twenty years ago," he whispered,
watching over her shoulder.

"Let me try something else." She hurriedly clicked
at the keys. "Wait, I've got it." He watched her type
in Keyword: Inez. What came up on the screen was a
list of patients under Genesis Project. She scrolled
down to Wellington, Holly. File: Current.

"What is the Genesis Project?" Slade asked.

"I have no idea." She moved the cursor through the
list. Norma Curtis. Genesis Project. File: In storage.

He spotted another name. Patty Dunn. Genesis Project. File: Current.

Pharmacist Jerry Dunn's wife.

He wasn't surprised when Holly stopped the cursor
on Marcella Rawlins. Genesis Project. File: In storage.

"What do we all have in common?" Holly whispered, turning to look at him.

"I wish I knew. My first guess would be infertility
if I didn't know better."

Outside in the hall, the footsteps grew closer.

Slade put his hand over Holly's on the mouse and
scrolled on down to the end of the list, stopping just
once. On the name Lorraine Vogel. Genesis Project.
File: In storage.

''Clear the screen,'' he said next to her ear, then quietly stepped to the door to remove the chair blocking it, hoping the woman he'd seen leaving the office hadn't forgotten something. But the sound of the footfalls went on past the door as Holly joined him.

He waited for a few moments to make sure the hallway was clear, then opened the door.

''You looked as if you'd seen a ghost when Dr. Parris mentioned your mother,'' she whispered as they headed for the exit again. ''What happened to her?''

He kept his voice down even though it appeared everyone had gone to lunch—even the woman who'd been at the front reception desk earlier.

''She was murdered twenty years ago by the son of the woman who supposedly drove her up here on Tuesdays. Lorraine Vogel.''

''The woman who was also in the Genesis Project file,'' Holly said.

He nodded at Holly's thoughtful expression. ''The thing is, my mother kept all of this a secret. Why is that? And why would she be coming to a fertility clinic in the first place? She had two twelve-year-olds.''

''Twenty years ago. And she was a Genesis Project patient,'' Holly noted. ''Like me.''

''Yeah,'' he said. ''That's what has me worried.'' What was the Genesis Project? And what did any of this have to do with their baby? Probably nothing. They were just wasting time here. All he wanted was to get out of this place. It felt even more dangerous than he'd first suspected—and he had no idea what there was to fear here.

They were almost to the exit, crossing the great expanse of marble that made up the massive foyer, when an older man in a white lab coat over an expensive gray suit stepped from a doorway, almost colliding with them. Behind him was Inez Wellington.

"Holly," the man said, a reprimand in his voice.

"Holly, you remember Dr. O'Brien," Inez said, not seeming that happy to see them, or at least not Slade.

"Inez." Holly sounded scared, and when she looked at Dr. O'Brien it was clear to Slade that she had never seen him before—that she could remember anyway.

A tall man with thick dark hair, a square face and small, dark eyes behind wire-rimmed glasses, the doctor ignored Slade and turned all of his attention on Holly.

"I thought you were checking in?" O'Brien said, his voice low and rough as sandpaper and about as warm.

Holly shook her head. "I've changed my mind."

"Let's discuss this in my office. Alone," he said pointedly.

"There is nothing to discuss," Holly insisted.

"From what Inez has told me, I'm not sure you're capable of a reasonable decision at this point."

"I disagree," Slade said stepping between O'Brien and Holly. "I think she is more than capable of making a reasonable decision, and that decision is that she doesn't need your...help."

Slade heard Inez say something about commitment papers and court orders, but he'd already swept Holly past the doctor and Inez. He hit the massive front door, half afraid he'd find it locked. It flung open, the cold and snow hitting him in the face as he grabbed Holly's hand and bolted.

He could hear both O'Brien and Inez call after them. And another voice. Female. He glanced over his shoulder, thought he glimpsed Carolyn Gray step behind a column on the outside edge of the building entrance, but his attention was quickly drawn back to Dr. O'Brien. The doctor reached for something. An alarm went off.

"Run!" he yelled to Holly over the clamor.

The sky had darkened to gunmetal gray, huge floating snowflakes fell around them like confetti.

He and Holly reached the pickup before he let himself look back again. To his surprise no white-coated bodybuilder types had come exploding out of the Institute.

Holly jumped into the cab and he slid in after her. The pickup started, almost to his amazement. He wasn't sure what lengths these people would go to. He told himself they needed Holly back under their control. She was starting to remember too much, and by now they had to know that.

He spun the pickup out of the parking lot, snow flying off the hood and windshield, and headed for the gate, expecting that would be where the doctor planned to stop them. Pushing down the gas pedal, he increased his speed as he raced down the narrow evergreen-lined road, pretty sure he could ram through the gate if it came to that.

One glance at Holly told him she was braced for just that. She was buckled in, both hands on the dash, a look of incredulity on her face.

But to his amazement, the gate was open when he came around the bend. No guard tried to block his exit. No big orderlies tried to jump them.

Slade cruised out of the Institute's grounds and onto the highway, putting his foot to the metal as he watched in his rearview mirror, unable to believe their luck. No, not luck, he thought as the pickup put distance between them and Evergreen Institute. Dr. O'Brien had let them go. But why?

He glanced over at Holly. She too was looking back, obviously just as surprised. Then her gaze shifted to him and he had such a feeling of dèjá vu he almost drove off the highway. She was staring at him as if she'd never seen him before.

Chapter Twelve

"Holly?" Slade let out a curse as he met her gaze. They'd gotten to her. But how? The alarm? Or something O'Brien or someone else had said or done?

"Holly, you remember who I am, right?" Wrong.

She was gripping the door handle. He kept the speed up on the pickup, pretty sure she wouldn't be foolish enough to leap out, but not really sure *what* she'd do.

In his rearview mirror, he spotted a car coming up fast and swore.

She glanced back at the winding two-lane highway, then back at him. "What's going on?" She sounded only a little scared. "Rawlins?"

He shot her a look. "You called me Rawlins."

"Yeah," she said, still eyeing him strangely. "I've always called you Rawlins."

His heart hammered so hard in his chest he couldn't breathe. He stole another look at her. What he saw almost floored him. He let out a laugh. "Everything's just...fine now." He stole another look at her. Wasn't it?

She gave him a tentative smile. "Did you just call me Holly?"

The car was gaining on them, its cornering abilities

far exceeding the pickup's, especially in the middle of a snowstorm. He didn't dare go any faster. He was having enough trouble keeping his eyes on the road in this storm—and on the rearview mirror and Holly.

"You like the name?" he asked, praying he was right about who was sitting in the passenger seat next to him.

She smiled. God, but he'd missed that sexy, teasing, full-of-life smile. "It had better be your new name for me—and not just a slip of the tongue. Holly? I guess it's appropriate since you found me on Christmas Eve. Does have a nicer ring than Janie Doe."

He shook his head, grinning like a fool. Holly was back. His Holly. All he wanted to do was stop the pickup and take her in his arms. But that wasn't an option at the moment. The car was right behind them now. Something silver and sporty, like the BMW Dr. O'Brien drove.

"You know, I feel as though I've missed something here," she said, glancing nervously back at the car, then at him. "You sure everything is all right?"

"Yeah, what's the last thing you remember?" The car was trying to come around him on a solid yellow line.

"You in the shower."

He almost drove off the road.

"Don't tell me *you* don't remember?"

"Oh yeah." His heart was threatening to burst from his chest. "*Where* were we getting ready to go?"

"As if you don't remember. Your sister Shelley's. Dinner with Norma and the chief. You'd been grousing about going all day."

My God. She thought it was February 26 of last year, the day he came out of the shower not only to find her long gone, but his money and the files from his office gone as well.

"Right," he said, trying to keep the shock from his voice and his eyes on the road and the car behind them. The car made another attempt to pass, but backed off. A straightaway was coming up and Slade knew he wouldn't be able to keep the car from coming alongside him.

"You left the shower to dry your hair. The phone rang." He looked over at her, realizing now that was when someone had gotten to her. "By the way, who was that on the phone?"

She frowned. "That's funny. I can't remember."

The straightaway was just ahead. He reached across to the glove box and pulled out his weapon.

"Okay, now you're scaring me," she said. She bit at her lower lip. "Rawlins, are those the people who are trying to kill me?"

"Maybe, sweetheart. I need you to get down and stay down, okay?" He couldn't help but take another look at her, afraid it might be his last. The irony of it poleaxed him. He'd finally gotten her back, and, in the blink of an eye, he could lose her again.

He rolled down his window, snow pelting him. He squinted, one hand on the wheel, the other holding his weapon, as he watched the car come up his side of the pickup like a bullet, the driver hidden behind tinted windows. His trigger finger twitched. They weren't taking Holly from him. He'd kill them all if that's what it took.

He started to raise the gun, but then realized it wasn't Dr. O'Brien's car. His car hadn't had tinted windows.

The car seemed to hesitate for one heart-thundering moment next to the pickup, then sped on past, disap-

pearing into the snowstorm. He watched it go and
slowed the pickup, realizing he was shaking all over.

Whoever was behind this hadn't come after them
because obviously they'd accomplished what they'd set
out to do. Zap Holly. Take away her memory. Again.

But that meant they didn't see him as a threat. Probably because basically, he had nothing. Some pills that
Inez could say she knew nothing about. A blood typing
that proved nothing. And a woman with a shaky mental
history and no memory. He had zip and they knew it.

But he had Holly. Or did he?

"Holly?"

Her head popped up from where she'd hunkered
down in the seat.

He pulled off onto the first side road, cut the lights
and turned to her. She flew into his arms and he hugged
her to him as if there were no tomorrow. The way
things were going, there might not be.

"RAWLINS, you act as if you haven't seen me in
weeks," she laughed, drawing back a little to look into
his face. It felt as if they were in a cocoon, the snow
falling silently around them, covering the pickup in
white.

"Feels more like months," he said, touching his fingers to her lips. "God, I've missed you."

"Rawlins." She laughed, then sobered. "You're serious."

He nodded. "There's something I need to tell you."

"It's bad, isn't it?" She braced herself for the worst.
"What did you find out about me?"

"We can't stay here," he said starting the pickup.

"Rawlins, tell me what it is."

"I'll tell you on the way."

She listened, watching the snow fall hypnotically down from the heavens as he drove down the mountain. At first it felt as if he was talking about someone else. She would never steal files from him, let alone money. Nor could months have gone by. It was impossible.

But on the outskirts of Dry Creek, she began to see the Christmas lights. Too many of them for February. And this was Slade Rawlins, a man she trusted with her life. With her love.

"We had a baby together?" she asked in awe, her voice breaking. "A little girl?"

He pulled over at the edge of town as if suddenly realizing he didn't know where to go or what to do. "We can't go back to Shelley's. Or to my office or apartment. They'll probably be waiting for us. We can catch a flight from Butte." He started to turn the truck around.

She stopped him, shocked that he'd think she would run away. "We have to find her. We can't leave until we do."

"Holly," he said, killing the engine to turn to her. "You don't know what these people are capable of."

"Don't I, Rawlins? They stole our baby. They drugged me. They made me marry some crazed scientist. They messed with my mind and memory. I'm not about to let them keep my baby."

"Holly, they could have already—"

"They wouldn't hurt her," she said, believing it. "They went to too much trouble to get her."

She could see he wasn't so sure about that, but she couldn't doubt it. She had to believe their daughter was alive. "I have to remember the birth—the voice you said I recognized. Take me to this Dr. Delaney. You said he worked for Evergreen. If they took my memory away, then he should know how to bring it back.''

''Or completely erase it. Do you realize what you're asking me?'' he demanded. ''I just got you back after all these months. Holly, we can't be sure our baby is still alive. You're asking me to jeopardize your life, your sanity. I can't do that.''

''Rawlins, listen to me,'' she said, reaching over to grasp his upper arm. ''I know you, remember? You're not the kind of guy who runs away. It's just not in you.''

''Holly.'' His voice cracked, his eyes filled with pain. ''I'm not the same guy, not after a year without you. I want our baby as much as you do. But just the thought of never being able to hold you, to make love with you—'' He was shaking his head, but she knew he could no more run from this than she could.

She cupped his face in her hands and kissed him tenderly on the lips. ''Trust me, Rawlins. We will make love again,'' she whispered. ''I promise you that.''

He closed his eyes and pulled her to him with a groan.

''God help us,'' he whispered.

Silently, she echoed his words, more afraid than she would ever let him know. But equally determined never to be the woman Rawlins had described to her, the woman it seemed she'd been for almost the entire last year.

SLADE WOULD RATHER have cut off his right arm than do it, but he started the truck and headed for Dr. Delaney's house.

''Why would someone want to brainwash me?'' Holly said beside him. ''I'm an artist, right? Who in

their right mind would want to brainwash an *artist?*
That would be even more useless than brainwashing a
private detective.''

He knew what she was trying to do. She'd always
joked when she was scared. And she had to be running
scared as hell right now. ''You're a great artist.''

He wanted to argue that they should drive to Butte,
find a hypnotherapist, see if the guy could get her memory back. But he knew he'd be wasting his breath.
Holly was too smart not to know that time was of the
essence. And Dr. Delaney might be the one person who
knew how to get her memory back quickly. But would
he? Even at gunpoint.

''So you've seen my work?'' she asked, looking nervously at the road ahead.

He thought of the painting she'd done of the birth.
''You have real talent, trust me.''

''Sounds like you're not the first man to say that to
me,'' she said. ''Tell me about Dr. Allan Wellington.''

He was saved by the ringing of his cell phone.
''Rawlins.''

''Slade, man, have I got news for you,'' Charley
said. ''Dude, don't go near this Evergreen place.''

''Too late for that. What have you got?''

''The place was started by a guy named Dr. Allan
Wellington as a fertility clinic—''

''Got that.''

''Then you already know about Dr. August Wellington, the headshrinker?''

Slade frowned, trying to remember where he'd seen
that name. Inez's. A plaque on the wall. Some award.
''No.''

''Man, he was just one of leaders in mind control

during World War II, *and* he was Allan Wellington's *father.*"

Slade looked over at Holly. "That makes a lot of sense. Was the old man connected with Evergreen?"

"You bet your best sneakers he was," Charley crowed. "But unofficially, of course."

So Allan could have learned the techniques from his father. "Did you find out anything on a Dr. O'Brien?"

"Not yet. Still checking. But if he's bad news, I'll get the dirt, man. You can count on me."

"What about Inez Wellington?"

"The headshrinker's daughter?" Charley asked. "Word I got, she's an old maid with an attitude." That about covered it. "Flunked out of medical school. But she *did* work with her father and brother, unofficially. Not much on her. Still digging."

"Listen, be careful. At least one person is dead and another missing and I suspect it's all connected."

"Always careful, man. That's the name of the game. Later, dude."

"Who's dead?" Holly asked the moment he clicked the phone off. "You haven't told me everything, have you?"

"Your midwife. She was killed in a car wreck just before you gave birth. Supposedly, it was an accident."

"So she wasn't one of the monsters," Holly said thoughtfully.

"No. But it's quite the coincidence she died before she was to assist your birth."

Holly nodded, still looking stunned by the news, but stronger than the Holly who'd stumbled up to his office on Christmas Eve.

And Carolyn Gray was missing, it seemed, but he

suspected she hadn't gone far. In fact, he'd sworn he saw her outside the Institute just minutes ago.

Dr. Delaney, it appeared as they neared the house, was home, and with luck, the doctor would be alone. Dr. Delaney lived just outside of town on a small hobby ranch. As Slade pulled into the drive, he noted that only one vehicle was parked out front. The doc's black Suburban.

A mongrel dog came out to meet them, barking as it ran alongside the pickup. Slade parked behind the doctor's car and asked, "You're sure about this?"

"Positive," she said and gave him a smile. "After everything you told me, Dr. Delaney must realize Evergreen's house of cards is falling fast. He'll want to help us."

"Yeah," Slade said checking the clip on his weapon. "Or kill us." Or kill him and zap Holly into another state of mind.

And yet, he still had no proof that anything was going on. Nor was he ready to involve the police. But he wasn't fool enough to go to Dr. Delaney without letting at least someone know where he was.

He dialed Chief Curtis's private number and got his answering machine. "I'm at Dr. Delaney's house. He has some tie-in with Evergreen and might be one of the people who has been using mind control on Holly. We're about to find out. Just want you to know in case you don't hear from me again."

Dr. Delaney opened the door before they reached it as if he'd been expecting them. Not a good sign. He didn't seem surprised to see them—or the weapon Slade held in his hand.

"Are you alone?" Slade asked.

Delaney nodded.

"You knew we were coming?"

"Heard all about it on the police scanner." Delaney pointed into his den.

Slade could hear the chatter, turned low. "Why would we be on the police scanner?"

"Someone broke into Evergreen Institute, stole confidential information and destroyed the lab. You were seen leaving the Institute. There's a warrant out for your arrest and a court order for Holly Barrows's recommitment. I just had a feeling I'd be seeing you."

Slade couldn't believe what he was hearing. And now Chief Curtis knew exactly where to find the two of them.

"We took nothing from Evergreen, and we certainly didn't destroy any lab," he said. "It's a lie."

"That's why you're waving a gun around." Delaney didn't seem upset though. Or worried that Slade would shoot him. The doctor looked questioningly at Holly.

"I understand we've already met," she said, extending her hand. "I'm one of the casualties of Evergreen Institute's mind-control program, the Genesis Project, but I have a feeling you already know that as well."

The words had the effect Holly had obviously been shooting for. Delaney looked more than surprised.

"Look, we know you're involved with the Evergreen Institute and the Genesis Project," Slade said.

Delaney didn't bother to deny it.

"To make a long story short," Slade said. "We were just at Evergreen. Someone zapped her. She can't remember the past year. Convenient, huh?" He waved the weapon in his hand. "Now you're going to help her remember the birth of her baby and the monsters who stole it. Then you can tell us about the Genesis

Project and why you used to take my mother to Evergreen.''

Delaney looked at Holly. "What do you mean by 'zapped?'"

"Mind control. It seems I've been taking Halcion mixed with equal parts hypnosis," she said.

"Halcion? Unless it was a very low dosage, you wouldn't have even been able to function."

"It sounds as if I just barely could," she said. "But then someone else was controlling me so I didn't need to think much."

"How do you know this?" Delaney asked, turning to Slade.

He shook his head. "It doesn't matter. As long as you undo it. I know you've worked with hypnosis and de-programming."

Delaney let out a sigh. "This isn't the same thing. If Holly's memory loss wasn't hypnotically induced, putting her under will do no good."

"I guess there is only one way to find out," Slade said, "but first let's search the house," he said motioning with the weapon.

The house did appear to be empty, just as Delaney said.

When they returned to the main floor, Delaney motioned to the den. "Come on in here," he said to Holly.

"I'm coming too," Slade reminded him.

"I never doubted it. But put the gun away. It won't be necessary."

"I hope not."

Delaney stepped over to the police scanner and turned it off, then closed and locked the door behind them.

"Why do you have a scanner?" Slade asked.

The doctor gave him a pitying look and said sarcastically, "I secretly work for the police." Delaney shook his head in disgust. "Have you always been so paranoid?"

"More so lately," Slade admitted.

"You can sit here," the doc said to Holly. "This might surprise you Slade, but even though I'm trying to retire, if there is an accident or some reason the hospital might need assistance, I still go in to see if I can be of help."

"I was just wondering," Slade said. "The bell ringer, the one you had outside my office, did he call you on Christmas Eve? Or Carolyn Gray?"

Delaney shook his head. "I don't know what you're talking about."

Slade narrowed his gaze at the doctor. "And why didn't you just lie when I brought Holly to you to be examined? If you'd told me she hadn't had a baby, I might have just dropped the case."

"I had no reason to lie," Delaney said. "I'd never seen her before and knew nothing about any of this, but I don't expect you to believe that." Delaney looked at him, obviously irritated. "I suppose it would be too much to ask you to sit over there." He pointed to a spot off to Holly's right. "If I stand any chance of helping, you can't distract her in any way."

Slade nodded and took the seat Delaney suggested, but kept the revolver out, resting on his thigh, ready. He listened for any sound beyond the room, recalling how the doctor had locked the door behind them and the dog was outside. It would bark if anyone came around, warn them in time.

Delaney dimmed the lights, put on some soft music and took a chair facing them. Slade watched the doctor take Holly's hands in his. "Try to relax. Hypnosis is a state of increased suggestibility and concentration," he began, his voice low and soft.

"Under hypnosis you never relinquish your free will," he said, then looked over at Slade. "Hypnosis works on suggestion, but as with its use in weight loss or quitting smoking, it takes repeated attempts, and even then it is only viable if the patient accepts the suggestion. Although it is widely used, the success rate over a long period of time is poor."

Got the message, Slade said with a look.

Dr. Delaney turned his attention back to Holly. "Relax. Try to clear your mind. Make your mind peaceful. Quiet. Serene."

Slade rubbed the back of his neck. The room was almost too warm. He tried to focus outside the room, listening for the dog to bark, listening for any sound that might mean they were no longer alone.

"Holly," Delaney continued softly, as melodic as the faint music he had playing. "Hear only the sound of my voice, the sound of your own breathing. In and out. In and out. That's it. I'm going to help you to remember everything. You do want to remember, don't you?"

She nodded slowly.

Remember.

Slade shifted in his seat, still holding the weapon on his thigh, wondering if he hadn't heard the dog bark. Delaney shot him a look of warning and motioned for him to be quiet.

"Concentrate," Delaney said. "Hear only the sound of my voice. Nothing else matters. Just the sound of my voice and what I am going to tell you."

Slade let his attention shift back to Holly and Dr.

Delaney's voice, the music now almost part of the room.

He watched Delaney, spellbound, as the doctor's voice dropped in the darkened room. Slower and slower, softer and softer came the flow of words until the beat of the words seemed to match the beat of his heart.

Remember.

Remember.

The weapon slipped from his hand, fell in slow motion to the floor, hitting, but without sound. Slade thought about picking it up. Then lost the thought.

Chapter Thirteen

Remember.

Remember.

At the sound of Dr. Delaney's voice, Holly came awake in an instant, but she didn't move, barely breathed. With her eyes still closed, she tried to remember. Some of last year came to her as if it had never been missing.

But not the birth of her baby. It was just as elusive as it had been before, she realized with aching disappointment.

She started to open her eyes, but stopped at the sound of Delaney's voice again.

"You probably won't believe this, but I'm doing you a favor," Delaney said, off to her left.

She held her breath, wondering who he was talking to, afraid to open her eyes and find out. She realized she was sitting on something hard and cold and damp. From the air around her, she was no longer in the doctor's warm den and she knew without looking that that was a very bad sign.

"You really made a mess of things this time," Delaney said.

She could hear him moving around on the concrete

floor, the scrape of his soles. He stopped directly in front of her. Her heart thundered so loudly in her chest she thought for sure he would hear it. She waited, afraid he knew she was awake.

"This is the best I can do for you," Delaney said.

She felt more than heard something drop beside her. Whatever it was hardly made a sound when it hit, but kicked up the cool, damp musty air. She felt her hair move. Her eyes flickered. She tried desperately to breathe slowly and not move. Not blink.

Then she heard him move away. She opened her eyes to slits and peered through her lashes, willing herself not to move another muscle.

She saw Slade sitting directly across from her and her breath caught in her throat. His eyes were open. He was staring at her, but it was clear he wasn't seeing anything! Oh my God! A scream rose up her throat—

Then she saw his chest rise and fall, rise and fall. He was alive. She closed her eyes for a moment, trying to dam the tears of relief.

She could hear Delaney off to her left working on something metallic. It clicked as he moved.

Cracking her eyes open a little, she tried to see where she was and what Delaney was doing without moving her head. She and Slade were in a small concrete room with no windows. It would have felt like a basement if it wasn't for the battery-operated lamp overhead and the massive steel door that Delaney was standing by. In the middle of the door was a mechanism that looked like the lock on a vault. Only the dial was on the *inside!* And Delaney was turning it.

He stopped, as if sensing her watching, and started to turn in her direction. She closed her eyes and willed herself not to move. Instinctively, she knew he was looking at her, watching her closely. It was all she could do not to hold her breath. Not to twitch.

Her mind raced. She'd seen a place like this before when she was a kid. Panic filled her. It was a bomb shelter—like the one her grandparents had built in the nineteen-fifties. Why would Delaney put them—

She heard the metallic *click, click, click* and opened her eyes. He was planning to seal them up in here! She frantically looked around for a weapon, seeing only the pile of blankets Delaney had dropped next to her earlier, as she scrambled to her feet and rushed at him.

Dr. Delaney looked back in surprise, his hand on the door.

"No!" She threw herself at him, but he'd seen her coming. He slammed the door. It clanged shut, a deafening, final sound, just as she hit it. "No!" she screamed, her cry echoing in the tiny room.

She pounded on the door, knowing it was senseless. Pressing her palms and her cheek against the cold steel, she listened, thinking she might be able to hear if Delaney was still out there. As if from that, she could determine whether or not he'd ever be back.

She tried to turn the knob, but it wouldn't move. She leaned against the door and closed her eyes. No one knew they were down here. No one knew what Dr. Delaney and the rest of them had been doing to her mind for over a year. And no one knew about her baby. Her—and Slade's—baby girl.

And now Slade was gone into that other world. And she had no idea how to reach him. She'd never felt so alone. Or so defeated.

Remember.

Remember.

Slade woke to a loud clang. He blinked, instantly

aware that he was no longer in Dr. Delaney's den and
that he no longer had his weapon.

Remember.

Remember.

He sat up, cobwebs of confusion clouding his
thoughts. A voice inside his head kept repeating: *remember.* And yet he could remember little of what had
happened in Delaney's den.

He blinked again, taking in the concrete room, the
steel door and the woman standing in front of it.

"Holly?" he asked, his heart in his throat at just the
thought that he might have lost her. Again.

She spun around, her eyes flying open. "Rawlins!"
And then she was on the floor and in his arms.

He cupped her head in his hand as she pressed her
face to his chest, his arm crushing her to him.

"I thought you were gone." She was crying, her
head against his chest. "I thought I'd lost you the way
we'd lost each other last year."

He rocked her, turning his face up to the heavens, a
silent prayer of thanks on his lips. Wherever they were,
whatever they were locked inside, however much time
they had, they had each other right now.

He lifted her face, wiped her tears with the pads of
his thumbs, as she stared at him, her eyes wide and
dark. She seemed to hold her breath. He imagined that
he could hear her heart pounding beneath her breast,
but he knew he couldn't have heard it over his own.

"Holly." He said her name like a prayer. Like a
promise. "Holly." He gently touched her face, cupping
her cheek in the palm of his hand, thumbing away her
tears, then trailing across the silken skin to her lips, her
full, lush lips. She kissed the pad of his thumb, her
eyes locking with his.

He felt a stab of desire so sharp it cut to the heart of him. The heat moved through him, a hot lava flow that ignited him. Drawing her onto his lap, he dropped his mouth to hers, opening her, entering her as her lips parted in invitation. He cradled her head in his hands, deepening the kiss, feeling the aroused throb of her pulse through his fingers, the sudden spurred quickness of her breath against his mouth, her small gasp as he drew her lower lip into his mouth, caught it between his teeth.

Her eyes filled with liquid fire, lighting up like stars. Or sparks. He thought his heart would burst from his chest.

"I've missed you, Rawlins," she whispered breathlessly against his mouth. "I'd forgotten how much."

HOLLY TREMBLED at the look in his eyes. He buried his hand in her hair and pulled her down onto the blankets for his kiss. His mouth, his wonderful mouth, moved from her lips down her throat, leaving a trail of fire across her skin. "Rawlins," she whispered, feeling an urgency.

He opened her blouse, baring her breasts, his breath warm, as he moved down her, pushing aside her clothing to make way for his mouth as if he too couldn't bear them being apart another moment. His lips found her breast, provoked her nipple to a hard, pulsing point.

She arched against his mouth, her body melting against him. Then she drew him back up to her. His gaze locked with hers. They needed no words. Only this coupling of bodies, of hearts. A bonding that affirmed life.

She fumbled to free the buttons on his shirt in a

desperate demand to feel his warm bare skin against hers. Pushing back the cloth, she flattened her palms again the solid heat of his chest, breathing in the scent of him, the feel of him. He groaned and pulled her down, surrendering to her touch as his mouth took hers again, and they struggled out of their clothing, their lips never parting. She tore at his clothing, needing nothing between them. Needing him.

And then they were naked. Her body melded with his, heat to heat, her skin alive from his touch, wet from his kisses. He lifted his mouth from hers, his gaze connecting with hers, then he entered her, filling her, fulfilling her, finally bringing her home.

SLADE ROLLED HER onto her back on the thick pile of blankets when it was over and looked down into her eyes, a smile on his lips. "You are the most desirable, beautiful, enchanting woman I have ever met."

She smiled up at him. "Rawlins," she said with a satisfied sigh, "You don't get out enough."

He lay down beside her, holding her in his arms. "I'm just so glad you're back."

"Rawlins, we're locked in a bomb shelter," she said.

"I see that." But all he saw was her, her wonderful face and eyes and lips, and her silken body next to his. He took her hand and kissed the tips of her fingers.

"It appears there's a timer built into the door."

"I understand the concept," he said. He didn't dare let himself think about the fact that they were trapped, powerless to do anything about their baby or the world outside that steel door. He didn't know how much time they had. Only that they had it together. He didn't plan to spend that time worrying about what could have been or losing his mind over something he could do nothing about.

"The door isn't going to open until that timer goes off," she said. "And maybe not even then."

"Uh-huh." He ran his fingers from her palm up the inside of her arm to her elbow.

"You don't seem too upset about that."

"Holly, I'd break down that door for you if I could. Since I can't…" He spooned her against him as he ran his fingers from her shoulder, down the long slope of her waist and up over her hip. "I spent the last year dreaming about having you in my arms again. Now that I do…I just want to make love to you until that door opens."

"What if it never opens?" she asked, sounding a little breathless as she turned in his arms to met his gaze.

He grinned. "I think you know the answer to that one." He drew her to him again.

HE WOKE with a start, not sure at first what had roused him from a sated sleep. The first thing he felt was Holly's warm body curled in his arms. Before that, he'd thought he'd only been dreaming. But it all came back in a flash and instinctively, he pulled her closer as he looked around to see what had awakened him.

He'd forgotten they were locked in a bomb shelter. He'd even forgotten to worry whether or not there was sufficient air. His plan had been to make love to Holly until hell froze over. Or until they completely ran out of air in this steel-lined concrete box. Or until the door opened.

He sat up.

"What is it?" Holly asked sleepily.

"The door," he whispered. "It's open."

Chapter Fourteen

December 27

Holly sat up, drawing the blanket over her nakedness as she stared out into the dark beyond the open door. Without a word, Rawlins handed her her clothes and motioned for her to follow him. She half expected Dr. Delaney to appear at any moment in the opening. Or that the door would suddenly slam shut before they could reach it.

Neither happened. She hurried out of the bomb shelter to find a set of stairs leading up. Slade was pulling on his jeans. She quickly dressed and, taking the hand he offered her, let him lead her up the stairs, tiptoeing, quiet as mice.

The house seemed too quiet as Slade pushed open a door and they came out in the laundry room.

They stood for a moment, Slade obviously listening, his gaze warm on hers as if reminded of what they'd just shared. As if she could ever forget it.

She could see her own emotions mirrored in his eyes. Disbelief that they had found each other again. Fear that they might lose everything in the next few minutes. And hope, hope that they would still find their baby.

''My gun might still be in the den,'' he whispered.

She nodded, unsettled by the quiet of the house.

Up here, they could hear the howl of the wind outside, but nothing more. Where were the cops? Surely whoever Slade had called had gotten the message by now.

He motioned for her to follow him. As if she'd let him out of her sight for an instant if she could help it.

They moved through the darkness of the house, the white of the snowstorm giving them enough light through the undrawn drapes to navigate around the furniture and realized that it was a new day.

As they drew near the den, Holly felt a chill, as if there was a draft. The door to the den was partially open. Slade gave it a little shove, keeping back as though he thought he'd find Dr. Delaney waiting there with a weapon trained on them.

But Dr. Delaney wasn't sitting in the big chair by the fireplace. Nor behind the massive desk. Nor in the chairs she and Slade had occupied before.

Holly looked down and saw something at her feet that set her heart hammering. ''Rawlins,'' she whispered, terror in her voice. She pointed to the floor and the bloody partial footprint on the hardwood.

He quickly found another print, then another. They led down the hall toward the front door. She followed him and the prints, the air growing colder, the bloody footprints more distinct.

The front door was ajar. Dr. Delaney lay sprawled in a pool of blood at its base, his left arm caught in the door as if he'd tried to keep it from closing behind his killer.

"Oh, God," Holly cried as Slade knelt beside the doctor's inert body.

"Is he…?"

"Yeah, he's dead. He's been shot. I would suspect with my gun." Slade stood and turned to look at her.

"Why kill Delaney?" she whispered. "He was one of them, right?" A thought hung suspended between them. "Why didn't he tell them we were in the bomb shelter?"

She watched Slade open the door with the sleeve of his shirt, hesitate, then close it again. "My pickup's gone."

He checked Delaney's pockets then moved past her, headed back toward the den.

She followed him, not saying the one thing she knew they both were thinking. If these people would kill Dr. Delaney, what would they do to the little baby girl Holly had given birth to? "Rawlins, we have to call the police," she said as she followed him into the den.

"We can't, Holly," he said as he began to go through the desk drawers. "Even if they believed that we were locked in the bomb shelter at the time Delaney was killed, they'd hold us for questioning. It could take hours."

And they didn't have hours. That's what he was thinking.

"What are you looking for?" she asked.

"Keys to Delaney's Suburban, my weapon, any weapon," he answered, not looking up.

He slammed the drawers and headed for a set of cabinets on the opposite wall. She grabbed his sleeve as he started past. He cupped her cheek in his hand and she leaned into it, grasping his wrist, needing to feel the steady beat of his pulse, to assure herself they were still alive and there was still hope of finding their baby alive as well.

"I'll help you look," she said, letting him go. She could hear the police scanner now, turned so low the sound was like a moan. The room was warm, but she hugged herself for a moment to chase off the chill, then began to look around on top of the desk for Delaney's keys to keep from thinking about who had killed him and what those people would do next. Or why they hadn't come down to the bomb shelter and killed her and Slade. Several answers presented themselves. Either the killers hadn't known the two of them were down there. Or they couldn't get the door open.

If it was the latter, then they might be back to finish the job. She watched Slade search the drawers of the desk, noticing the way he used his shirtsleeve, leaving no prints, realizing they were both wanted now. Him by the law. Her by monsters and mad psychiatrists.

Her gaze was drawn to another sound in the room. The computer. It was on. Using her sleeve to cover her fingers, she touched the mouse.

The screen flashed on. She stared at the words typed there and said, "Rawlins, you'd better come here."

He was at her side in an instant.

"Look. I think it's a confession." It appeared Delaney had started to type it before he was killed. Whoever had murdered him must not have realized it because the computer had gone into standby mode, the screen dark.

"What the—" Slade read the words aloud.

To Whom It May Concern: In 1935, Hitler established a semi-secret breeding program called *Lebensborn* meaning the Fountain of Life. The main

function of *Lebensborn* was to provide racially
ideal women for breeding to members of the SS
and other selected men. Women were kidnapped
and children were separated from parents. Some
children were rejected. Some were placed with
other families and were brainwashed to believe
they were the offspring of these parents.

Slade stopped reading to glance over at Holly, his
eyes dark and troubled.
She nodded and swallowed as he continued,

Hitler's programs put the government in the po-
sition of controlling people's sex lives. "We reg-
ulate relations between the sexes. We form the
child," Hitler proclaimed. Selection, breeding and
elimination was the key.
   For more than thirty years, there has been a
modern-day *Lebensborn* operating right here, only
its methods are much more efficient, much more
covert and insidious. Using the brainwashing techniques his father had initiated, Dr. Allan Wellington started his own superior breed. He formed a
microcosm of what could be if babies were born
only to the best possible couples. His sights were
on the future of mankind. It wasn't until I became
involved with Carolyn Gray that I learned the extent of Dr. Welling—

The cursor blinked. The rest of the screen was blank.
"Sweet heaven," Slade whispered.
All Holly could do was stare at the screen. She
wanted to scream, to cry. "What does this mean? Is he
saying our child was part of some experiment to create

a master race? Or one of the ones rejected?'' Eliminated?

Slade shook his head as he pulled her to him and stroked her hair.

"But Allan is dead! How could he…"

"I don't know, Holly."

She pulled back to look at him. Of course, he was as stunned and scared as she was—and just as shocked by the possible ramifications. For more than thirty years? Slade's mother had been part of the Genesis Project. So had Holly. But at least his mother hadn't married the crazy doctor. But Holly had! Even if it had only been for a few days. She realized how lucky she was that he'd died when he had. How *had* she gotten that lucky? It seemed almost too convenient. She shivered.

"I'm not sure what any of this means," Slade said, "But let's not jump to conclusions, all right?"

She wished that were possible. She watched him move back to the cabinets he hadn't searched yet, unable to keep from thinking of babies that were deemed unacceptable.

Slade opened a cabinet and froze.

"What is it?" she asked, deathly afraid to find out.

He turned slowly, and she saw the mask he held in his hand. She recognized the monster face from the night of her delivery. "Delaney was one of them."

He threw down the mask. "Let's get out of here. If I have to, I'll hot-wire Delaney's Suburban." He stopped and turned to look back at her, realizing she wasn't following him.

She was still standing behind the desk staring at the words Delaney had written. Her movements seemed jerky as if she'd been somewhere cold for too long as she hit Print, then Save, and waited. When the machine finished printing, she folded the sheet and stuck it in her coat pocket and turned off the computer.

Only then did she look at him. "I'm ready."

SLADE WATCHED her movements. Cold, calculating, a hardness in her expression. An anger. A resolve. He recognized it because he felt it just as strongly as she did. Holly was a fighter, and he was thankful for that. A weaker woman wouldn't have made it this far.

He couldn't even comprehend the extent of the Genesis Project. For thirty years these people had been playing God. He concentrated on only one thought: stopping them. He held little hope of getting their baby girl back. He couldn't shake the horrible feeling that if it wasn't already too late—it would be soon.

Hadn't somebody once stated that the world will be saved by one or two people? He hoped he and Holly were enough. Then he realized, Allan Wellington had thought he was saving the world. Delaney and Carolyn Gray probably had thought they were, too.

Slade took Holly's hand as they passed Dr. Delaney's body and stepped out into what had become a raging blizzard. Wind whirled the falling snow, pelting them with stinging ice crystals that felt more like sand. Ice-cold sand.

"The garage," Holly yelled over the wind. She motioned to the detached garage and the disappearing tracks that led from it.

Why would Delaney have put a vehicle in the garage?

Slade took Holly's hand and ran through the drifting snow and cold to the side door of the garage. He felt around, found the light switch and flicked on the garage lamp. His pickup was sitting there, ice and snow melting beneath it, the keys in the ignition.

"Maybe Delaney really did put us into the bomb shelter for our own good," Holly said. "Maybe he was trying to protect us. Hide us, just like he did the truck. But if he wanted to help us, why didn't he just call the police?" she said, echoing his very thought.

"Because he was guilty as hell," Slade said, realizing Delaney might have been planning to confess on the computer then skip the country—leaving him and Holly the pickup and the confession.

He doubted they would ever know what Delaney really had planned for them. Holly climbed into the front seat of the pickup, and he hit the garage-door opener. He climbed behind the wheel. Delaney was dead. Carolyn Gray was out there somewhere. That still left one monster unmasked. Slade knew they had to find him—before the two remaining monsters found them.

He put the pickup in four-wheel drive and backed out into the storm.

Snow had drifted across the road, but he could still see distinct tracks where someone had broken a trail in—and out again. The elusive Carolyn Gray? Or the third monster? And what if there were others involved in this? How could there not be? And yet, he knew something like this couldn't have been kept a secret for more than thirty years unless only a select few knew.

"Rawlins?"

"Yeah?" He burst through the last drift and hit the snow-packed highway, headed for Evergreen Institute. That's where the answers had to be. Someone had destroyed the lab. Trying to destroy evidence?

He glanced over at Holly when she didn't say any

more, half afraid that he might have lost her again. "Holly?"

"I just remembered something. I was thinking about the bomb shelter...cold, damp, concrete places..." Her gaze swung to his in the glow of the dash lights. "I know where I delivered our baby!"

Chapter Fifteen

It was late enough that the hospital parking lot was almost empty. Slade put his arm around Holly's shoulders as they hurried through the snowstorm to the front door.

The admitting nurse wasn't at her desk. As a matter-of-fact, all hell seemed to be breaking loose. Holly saw Head Nurse Lander rush by, a grimace on her face. From down the hall came a familiar braying voice.

"Inez," Holly said, immediately moving toward the sound.

The door to Inez's room was open. Nurse Lander had pushed her way in and was trying to raise her voice higher than Inez's.

"What seems to be the problem here?" Nurse Lander was demanding.

Inez began telling her, but stopped abruptly at the sight of Holly and Slade.

"I'd like to see my sister-in-law alone, please," Holly said to Nurse Lander.

The head nurse looked so grateful that Inez Wellington had finally shut up, she just gave a curt nod and motioned for the other nurses to leave with her.

The moment the door closed, Inez said to Slade, "I thought I fired you."

Slade was moving around the bed to the side opposite Holly, who calmly demanded, "I want to know where my baby is."

Inez rolled her eyes. "Oh, you aren't going to start—"

Slade laid a hand on the older woman's shoulder. "She asked you where her baby was."

Inez's eyes glittered maliciously. "Dead. Just like my brother, the man you killed!"

"He died of a heart attack!" Holly said, trying to keep her voice down.

"There was nothing wrong with his heart. Nothing!" Inez spat. "Until he married *you*."

Holly shook her head. "He had to drug me to get me to marry him. What about that?" She waved away the question. "Evergreen. Tell me about his Genesis Project. Tell me about the babies. What did he do with the babies he stole from the mothers?"

Inez looked at her blankly.

"Dr. Delaney told us. I know what Allan was doing, using mind control to build what he considered a superior future generation." Inez started to protest, but Holly cut her off again. "Dr. Delaney is dead, but he left a confession."

Inez paled. The monitor beside her bed started to beep loudly. Slade reached over and unplugged it. "Whoever took over for your brother stole our baby. I don't think I have to tell you to what extremes we will go to get the truth."

Inez's eyes widened. She tried to ring for the nurse, but Holly grabbed the call button and moved it out of her reach.

A nurse stuck her head in the doorway, obviously alerted by the monitor suddenly going off.

"Everything's fine in here," Slade said, keeping a restraining hand on Inez's shoulder.

"Help me, you stupid bitch," Inez yelled at the nurse.

"My sister-in-law is a little distraught," Holly said. "Just give us a few moments to calm her down."

Inez started to protest, but the nurse shot Inez a call-*me*-a-bitch look and left, closing the door firmly behind her.

"You're going to kill me," Inez whined. "I'm a sick old woman."

"Yes, you are," Holly agreed.

Inez narrowed her eyes, anger making her nostrils flare. "My brother saw what was happening in the world. Stupid, lazy, ill-equipped people having child after child, children who would do nothing but become burdens on society, dependents of dependents, multiplying at staggering rates, the useless conceiving more of the useless."

Holly stared at her. "Who did he think he was that he got to decide who had children and who didn't? No wonder Delaney compared him to Hitler."

Inez looked shocked. "Allan was a brilliant doctor who was trying to save this planet. How dare you compare him to Hitler? My brother wasn't a racist. He was a realist."

"What did he do with the children?" Slade asked, his voice deadly low.

Inez turned her head to look at him. "The desirable ones got good homes with desirable parents who would provide the right kind of environment. It was the Wellington legacy to the future world," she said proudly.

"And the undesirable babies?" Holly asked, her voice barely a whisper.

Inez slowly turned to look at Holly again. "They were disposed of."

Holly felt her heart crush under the weight of the words. "Slade's and my baby? Which was it?"

"Do you even have to ask?" Inez said, seeming to have trouble breathing. She reached again for the call button to ring the nurse, looking small and weak in the large hospital bed.

Holly buzzed the nurse for her and dropped the call button on the bed beside Inez as she turned and walked away, afraid of what she'd do if she stayed a moment longer.

"Tell me who took over after Allan died," Slade demanded. "Tell me who is responsible for our baby's... theft."

"Go...to...hell," Inez wheezed.

"I will destroy the Wellington name, yours, your brother's and your father's," Holly heard Slade say to Inez. "The Wellington legacy will be a disgrace, dishonor and disgust."

"You won't live that long," Inez managed to utter. "And neither will Holly."

Then the hospital-room door closed, and Slade joined Holly in the hall. Holly could hear the clatter of a code-blue cart and the scurry of nurses. She didn't look back.

"We need to find the basement," she said, no longer sure she wanted to see where their baby had been born, but realizing she had to. She prayed it would make her remember something that would help them find their baby. If nothing else, she had to prove what the monsters had done and stop every last one of them once and for all.

SLADE FOLLOWED Holly down the hall, too shaken to speak. He'd wanted to throttle the truth out of the old woman, but he knew Inez would take it to her grave.

Holly had told him about her memory of the birth room. "It had to be close to the hospital, right? A room that was virtually soundproof, accessible and yet close enough that if something went wrong, they could get the mothers to the hospital quickly." He'd agreed. "What about under the hospital? My father was a bricklayer. He helped build the new hospital. I remember him telling me that they built the new one over the old one. Just like Seattle built over the city below it. It wasn't all that unusual back in those days."

Now all they had to do was find a way to access the old part because he believed Holly was on to something.

"I'm sure there is an outside entrance somewhere," she said now. "But there also has to be a way to access it from inside the hospital. A way to make it easy to bring patients in and out."

They found the door to the basement. It was locked. Of course. He pulled out his lock-pick kit. It only took a few moments while Holly stood guard. The door swung open and he pulled her onto the landing at the top of the concrete steps. Below them was nothing but darkness and cold.

Cold. Holly had been suffering from hypothermia, as if she had been outside.

"Carolyn Gray probably had a key," Holly said next to him.

"Yeah," he agreed as he fumbled around for a light

switch. A long line of lights blinked on, illuminating a short set of stairs. With Holly right behind him, he descended the steps to find a long hallway running north. At the end of the hall was another door.

It too was locked—but only temporarily. As it swung open, Holly let out a gasp. "This is it. The hallway I remember from my dream." She started down it, passing up several doors.

He hurried after her, passing rooms stuffed with boxes and old furniture.

"This part of the hospital isn't directly under the other," he said more to himself than Holly.

"Soundproof," Holly said. "No one would be able to hear a woman scream."

Her words sent a chill through him. He ached at the thought that Holly had given birth down here.

"Rawlins?"

They were almost at the end of the hall. He heard only that one word and the sound of Holly's voice breaking and knew she'd found something.

She stood in one of the doorways, her body rigid, her face pale.

He moved to look past her into the room. It was bare except for the large hospital bed at its center—and a hospital bassinet. It was obvious that the room had recently been cleaned.

She stepped in, then stopped. "This isn't the room," she said, turning to look at him, then her gaze moved past him to the last room, the one across the hall.

He could see from her expression that she was thinking the same thing he was. This would have been the room the other woman gave birth in. Holly moved past him, out into the hall. Slowly, she opened the last door. He heard her let out a small cry.

The room looked exactly like the other one, and he realized it too had been cleaned. There would be no evidence that Holly had given birth here. Nor any proof that the other woman had either.

"Is this the room?"

She nodded, but he couldn't see how she could be sure. The rooms looked identical to him.

He stood just inside the door, almost afraid to move, his heart pounding wildly as he watched Holly walk to the bassinet as though in a trance. He tried not to imagine what she must be reliving. The room was so cold, so remote. As he stared at the bassinet, he fought hard not to think about what had happened here. Or would happen again if they didn't stop it.

"Oh damn, Rawlins," he heard her say. He swung his gaze from the bassinet to her. She was standing beside the bed, staring up at the ceiling.

Slowly, he followed her gaze. The paint had cracked at the corner of the ceiling just above the bed, leaving dark lines in the shape of something unimaginable. A monster.

Behind him, he heard the distinct scuff of footsteps on concrete. He spun around, realizing he had no weapon.

Holly turned at the sound as well. A figure stood in the door. "Rawlins, that's the woman! The one from the cemetery!" The woman wore a blue housekeeper's uniform, her face ashen, her hands clutched over her chest as if in prayer. "Where is my baby?" Holly cried, lunging toward her.

The woman's eyes widened, then rolled back into her head. Slade barely reached her before she hit the floor. He caught her in his arms and carried her over to the hospital bed.

"That's her," Holly said, staring down at her. "She's not...dead is she?"

"No, she just passed out." The woman's name tag read Gwen Monroe. She appeared to be in her early thirties, but she could have been much younger. She was one of those women who had a lot of miles on her, and it showed in her face. Her hands were rough and red, the nails chewed to the quick. "Do you know her?"

Holly shook her head. "The first time I saw her was at the cemetery. That is, as far as I can remember."

Gwen Monroe. A housekeeper at the hospital. The hospital where both Holly and Gwen had given birth—only in an old deserted underground part of it.

The housekeeper's lashes flickered. She came fully awake and, with obvious fear, pushed herself up, backing across the bed away from them until she reached the wall. "Who are you?"

"Don't you know?" Holly said. "You gave me your baby."

The woman blanched, and, for a moment, Holly thought she would faint again.

"Where is my daughter?" Holly demanded.

Slade touched her arm. "Easy," he warned. "Ms. Monroe?" he coaxed. "We aren't going to hurt you," Slade continued in that same soothing voice. "We're looking for our baby, the one Holly gave birth to the same night you gave birth to your son down here."

What were they doing—good cop, bad cop?

"I don't know nothin'!" Gwen Monroe said.

"Would you rather talk to the police?" Holly asked.

Panic washed over Gwen's features. "You can't prove nothin'."

"You're wrong about that," Slade said calmly.

"The doctors upstairs took blood from both Holly and your baby Halloween night. That blood will prove that the infant is yours."

"Blood's not conclusive evidence," Gwen said, obviously just repeating what someone had told her.

"But DNA is," Holly said.

The woman blinked.

Holly continued, "It would mean digging up the baby's grave, but we are prepared to do that if you don't—"

"No," Gwen Monroe cried. "I don't want him dug up."

"Who contacted you about giving up your baby?" Slade asked.

It had to have been nurse Carolyn Gray, but Holly knew Slade just wanted to confirm it.

"She said I better not say nothin'." The woman's face crumbled. "My baby, he quit movin'. She checked and said he was dead and would have to come out. That I'd have to bury him." Tears streamed down her face. "I don't have no money. I got two other kids, no husband. She said she would help me. Get him a decent burial. Let him be somebody and that I would get money to help my other kids." She looked up at them, her gaze pleading with them to understand.

"Who was she, this woman who helped you?" he asked.

"Lorraine. Lorraine Vogel," she said, her voice barely audible.

Holly stared in shock. The woman Dr. Parris had talked about. The mother of the young man who'd killed Slade's mother.

"How do you know Lorraine?" Slade asked with obvious shock.

"She works here as a nurse," Gwen said.

"What did they do with *my* baby?" Holly asked.

Gwen shook her head. "I don't know. I was real sick."

"But you knew they'd switched your baby with mine," Holly persisted. "That's why you were at the grave."

Gwen looked scared. "Not till later. She told me not to think about it. Not to go there. But I had to. Just that one time, really."

"Who delivered your baby?" Slade asked.

She shook her head. "They had on masks. Lorraine said it was better that way, then I couldn't get in no trouble." She looked up at Slade. "I can't give the money back. I ain't got it no more."

"How much did they pay you?" he asked.

"Two thousand dollars." There was awe in her voice.

"You don't have to give the money back," he assured her. "What were you doing down here today?"

"Sometimes I just come down here. I can't go to the cemetery. So I just come down here."

THE WIND howled on the outskirts of town, rocking the pickup and blowing snow into deep drifts. After her son's confession and suicide, Lorraine Vogel had moved from Slade's old neighborhood to a rundown stretch of windblown, low-rent space behind an old motel and gas station on the edge of town.

"*This* is where she lives?" Holly asked in surprise as she stared through the blowing snow.

According to the address in the phone book—and the rusted, dented mailbox—Lorraine lived in an ancient small trailer at the back, with old tires holding down the roof to keep it from blowing off.

Slade pulled behind the abandoned motel and they got out, fighting the wind and the airborne snow as they waded out to the trailer. He pounded on the rusted metal, the wind whistling through the tread-bare tires on the roof, the air thick with snow.

Lorraine Vogel opened the door, a gray sweater wrapped around her boney shoulders. She didn't seem surprised to see him.

"I'm Slade Rawlins—"

"I know who you are." Her voice was hoarse, her body was small and thin. She looked eighty but would have been closer to sixty by his estimation. He could see her in a Halloween monster mask at the foot of Holly's bed. As frightening as the other two monsters even for her age and frailty.

"I'm here about Gwen Monroe," he said and realized she must have known that as well.

She nodded, unhappiness stamped in a lifetime of lines on her face. He wondered if the woman had ever known peace. He'd heard that Roy's father had taken off on her long before the boy was born, long before her real problems with Roy had begun.

She stepped aside to let them in. "What other reason would you have for being here?" she asked, sounding a little drunk.

The trailer was dark and cold, a woodstove working futilely in one corner. Slade spotted an almost-empty bottle of cheap bourbon sitting on the kitchen counter with an empty glass next to it.

"This is Holly Barrows," he said.

Lorraine gave her the once-over and dismissed her. If the name rang any bells, Lorraine's expression didn't give it away. But maybe the older woman had already recognized her.

Lorraine motioned to the couch, a lumpy, discolored blob slumped against the wall of the living room. He and Holly chose to stand as Lorraine took the chair in front of the woodstove, her thin form molded into the cushions of the chair from the long hours she must spend in it in front of the fire.

"Gwen told us about the deal you got her for her baby," Slade said, wasting no time.

Lorraine made no sign that she'd heard him. She seemed to be watching the fire through the cracks in the old cast-iron woodstove as if lost in thoughts of her own.

"I need to know about the other baby, the one Holly gave birth to," he continued. "Whoever else helped you deliver those babies, I think they're the same people who killed my mother. I believe they killed your son too. But you probably know more about that than I do."

Still she didn't move, didn't respond, as if she'd lost interest years ago in her son's guilt or innocence or her own.

"Dammit, Lorraine, these people have Holly's baby. My baby."

Her head turned slowly, her eyes narrowing as she looked at him. "Your baby?" She seemed confused and he saw that she was drunker than he'd first thought.

"Please, help us, Mrs. Vogel," Holly pleaded. "I was told I had given birth to Gwen Monroe's stillborn—but you know I had a baby girl. What happened to her?" Holly's voice broke, and Slade could see her fighting tears. "Please, we don't care about anything but getting our baby back."

Lorraine was staring at Holly, her eyes rheumy and moist in the firelight. "I never know where the babies go."

"Who does?" Slade asked.

She wagged her head, her neck seeming too weak to hold it anymore.

"Lorraine, I don't want to have to call the police—"

Her look was pitying. "As if anyone can keep history from repeating itself. I was there the night you and your sister were born. That's when he got the idea."

"Wellington?" Slade guessed.

She nodded, and tears filled her eyes and splashed down her cheeks seemingly without her notice.

"I know you and my mother were part of a special project at Evergreen Institute, Genesis," Slade prodded. "What is it?"

"Through Genesis he will live forever," she said and smiled. "You probably thought Allan was dead."

Slade was trying to decide if Lorraine was drunk. Or nuts.

Holly knelt at the old woman's feet and took Lorraine's hands in her own. "Tell me about my baby, please."

Lorraine shook her head; it wobbled, then drooped to her chest.

"Slade, I think she's taken something!" Holly was on her feet, moving to the liquor bottle. He heard the rattle of an almost-empty pill bottle as he moved to Lorraine's side.

The older woman seemed to rally for a moment. He could hear Holly on the phone calling 911, but he doubted the paramedics would be able to get here in time.

"Lorraine, for God's sake tell me how I can find my baby," he said, not sure she could even still hear him.

Her eyes glazed over, opaque as cataracts, her mouth opened, the words that fell out almost undistinguishable. But he heard enough to make him lurch back in shocked horror.

He stared at the woman, wanting to cry out his frustration. His rage. But it would have been a waste of words. Lorraine Vogel was gone.

"The paramedics are on their way," Holly said. "Rawlins, this prescription is today's date. I think she took almost the entire bottle."

He felt for a pulse and shook his head.

"My God, no!" Holly cried. "She was our last hope."

"No," he said, refusing to believe that as he rose. He was still shaking from what Lorraine had told him. It was worse than he'd first expected. So much worse.

"Why would she kill herself? She couldn't have known we were coming here," Holly said.

"Maybe Dr. Delaney warned her. Or Carolyn Gray. Or maybe she knew Carolyn would be coming after her."

He could feel Holly's gaze on him. "What did she tell you? Please, you have to tell me."

He tried to find the words. "She told me my mother was infertile and that my life, my sister's and my children's lives would always be in danger because of my genes." He swallowed, his mouth tasting of bile.

"Your genes?" Holly said.

"It seems Allan was fathering babies at Evergreen Institute by using artificial insemination and mind control on unsuspecting women who believed they were infertile."

"Rawlins, what are you saying?"

"The program didn't end with his death."

Her eyes widened in obvious confusion and shock.

"He froze his own sperm and whoever took over his 'master plan' took over the baby-making and the baby elimination."

"But not our baby," she whispered, fear making her look like a deer caught in headlights. "Our baby had a dimple. Tell me between that and the birthmark there is no way—"

"There is no way," he said. "But at first I thought, if my mother was part of the Genesis Project—"

"But then you remembered the Rawlins' dimples," she said.

"Yeah. Joe Rawlins was my father, and I'm the father of your baby." So what did the Genesis Project have to do with him? And his and Holly's baby? It all came back to his mother. If she really was infertile... What bothered him was that he couldn't remember any photos of his mother pregnant. He'd looked at all the albums last night and right now, he couldn't remember even one of his mother pregnant with him and Shelley.

He shook his head, trying to shake off the horror of what the old woman had told him. "Lorraine said my mother was too smart for her own good."

"You think she figured out what Allan was doing?" Holly asked in a hushed whisper.

"Maybe. I don't believe she wanted more children. But she might have pretended she did if she'd discovered something odd going on up at Evergreen."

"But why wouldn't she tell your father?"

He shook his head. "Maybe because she knew he'd try to stop her."

He glanced around the trailer. They had to search it

before the paramedics arrived, because he and Holly had to be gone by then. He began going through drawers, while Holly dumped out the contents of Lorraine's purse on the couch and started sifting through them.

He found the photograph of Roy Vogel first. It was a shot of the boy at about five. He was standing beside his mother, both Roy and Lorraine were smiling into the camera, although even then Roy looked too intent.

There was another photograph in the drawer; this one rubber-banded to a worn bank book.

Carefully, Slade slipped the photo from beneath the rubberband, his fingers shaking with revulsion. It was a photograph of Roy, again at about age five. The boy was sitting on a man's lap, the man holding him the way a man would hold his son. The man in the photo was Dr. Allan Wellington. "Sweet heaven."

"Slade?" Holly said behind him. She held up a mask, exactly like the third one from her painting. "She was there."

The three monsters. Dr. Delaney. Carolyn Gray. Lorraine Vogel. And now two of them were dead. He thought he should feel something. Relief. Something. He just felt sick.

He handed her the photo without a word and opened the bank book, shocked by the amount. Lorraine Vogel was a rich woman, and Slade had a pretty good idea how she'd come by most of the money.

He turned to look at Holly. She had paled, her hand trembling as it held the picture. She glanced at the bank book. "Why would she live like this if she had all that money?"

Slade shook his head. He could hear the whine of an ambulance in the distance. Hurriedly, he stuffed the photos and the bank book into his coat pocket.

"I found these." Holly held up a large ring of keys. "She still works at Evergreen. Wanna bet there's a key on here?"

He took the key ring from her, his gaze meeting hers.

"Don't even think about trying to talk me out of it, Rawlins," Holly said. "I'm going with you to Evergreen. These people drugged me, made me think I was losing my mind, they stole my memory and they stole my baby before I even got to hold her—" Holly's voice broke, but a steely resolve honed among the tears in her eyes. "No matter how this ends, I plan to be there. That is where Carolyn Gray has to be—where the Genesis Project began."

One look at her and he knew arguing would be a waste of time. "We have to make one stop on the way."

As they left he glanced at Lorraine. He hoped she was with Dr. Allan Wellington again, someplace real hot.

Chapter Sixteen

Slade drove past Chief L. T. Curtis's home, not surprised to see that the cop's car wasn't there. He parked down the street and looked over at Holly.

"Rawlins?" Holly asked, sounding worried. "You aren't thinking you're going to leave me here, are you?"

His gaze met hers, all their hopes and dreams captured in that one look. He had thought about having the chief lock her up. That's the only way Slade knew he wouldn't worry about her. The truth was, however, he feared Curtis would put them both behind bars. For leaving the scene of a murder, if nothing else. By now the chief would have been out to Dr. Delaney's.

That was one reason Slade had no intention of going near the police station. If there hadn't been a warrant out for his arrest earlier, he was pretty sure there would be now, if he knew the chief.

"With Carolyn Gray still on the loose, I'm not about to go out to Evergreen Institute without some sort of backup," he assured her. "We'll tell Norma. She can contact the chief after we've left."

"Our baby girl's alive," Holly said. "There has to be something at Evergreen, some record of where we can find her. I feel it.'' She placed her hand over her heart, her eyes shining.

He nodded. He couldn't argue with a woman's heart—even if he'd wanted to.

"YOU JUST MISSED L.T.,'' Norma said when she opened the door, obviously surprised to see them. "He's worried to death about the two of you.''

"I figured as much,'' Slade said. "You remember Holly?'' Norma nodded and smiled, holding out her hand. "We met last year.''

"Yes, I remember,'' Holly said.

Norma ushered them into the living room. "Can I get you something to drink? I still have a few of those sugar cookies left, Slade.''

"No. We don't have time for that. There's something I need to tell you.''

She offered them a seat and Slade poured out everything they knew, from Holly's mind control to the monsters stealing her baby to Dr. Allan Wellington's superbabies and Dr. Delaney's and Lorraine's involvement and subsequent deaths.

Norma stared at him. "It's all so…unbelievable.''

"What is the Genesis Project that you and my mother and Lorraine Vogel were involved in at Evergreen Institute?'' he asked. "I know you were a patient there.''

"I told you that. L.T. and I were trying to have children.''

"But Dr. Allan Wellington couldn't help you?'' he asked.

"You know that, too. But I don't know anything about a Genesis Project. Nor did I know about Dr. Wellington's…superbabies.''

"So you were infertile?" Slade asked, remembering what Lorraine had said about his mother.

"No." She seemed to hesitate, looking at him as if trying to gauge how much he knew. "I came close once, but the babies were stillborn."

Babies? "Twins?"

She must have realized her slip. While she must have known that it would have been common knowledge she had been pregnant, not everyone knew it had been twins.

He stared at her, hearing the echo of Lorraine's words about history repeating itself, hearing the chief say he was sterile, hearing his own heart banging against his rib cage. "Do you have a photo of my mother when she was pregnant?"

Norma turned white, all the color bleaching from her face in an instant, and he knew. Should have always known. It had been right there in front of him the whole time.

"Who was the father of your babies?" he asked, his tone as cold and hard as the look he gave her. "I know it wasn't L.T. because he told me he was sterile."

She opened her mouth, then closed it. Tears filled her eyes. He watched her fight the inevitable. "Your father."

Slade squeezed his eyes shut. He wanted to put his fist through the wall. "And I was afraid my *mother* was having an affair," he ground out. He opened his eyes, fighting hard not to lose his temper. Lose his sanity. He felt Holly behind him, felt her hand squeeze his shoulder as she moved to stand behind his chair.

"You don't understand," Norma pleaded. "I did it for your mother. It was her idea."

"For you to have children by my father?" Slade

glared at her. "He was the man you were in love with, wasn't he? Did my mother know *that?*"

Norma said nothing, dropping her gaze in answer.

He shook his head, trying hard to make sense of all of it. So many lies. So many deceptions. But what did it have to do with his and Holly's baby? "What do you know about Holly's and my baby?"

"Slade, I swear to you on your father's grave that I didn't even know the two of you had a child together," Norma cried.

"Where were Shelley and I born?" he asked.

"In the hospital. The old underground part."

He felt Holly's hand tense on his shoulder.

"Dr. Wellington and Lorraine delivered you," Norma was saying. "Your mother was there. She pretended to be pregnant during the nine months. It wasn't that unusual back then for a woman to fake a pregnancy. There was a stigma to adoption. And infertility."

"That's why there weren't any photos of my mother pregnant, because everyone close to her knew it was a lie," he said, more to himself than to her. Was that the secret his mother had begged Aunt Ethel not to tell? Not about an affair. Not about Evergreen. But about the biggest lie of all. Except Joe Rawlins was in on this, he realized. It had to be another lie, this one his mother's own.

He felt Holly's hand, warm and reassuring. "My father agreed to this?"

"Not at first. But yes. He would have given your mother anything."

"Shelley doesn't know, does she?"

"No. How could she?"

"What about the chief?" Slade asked.

Norma seemed to hesitate again. "He knew."

"He was against it?" Slade guessed. "But you did it anyway, and we both know why. Obviously, the chief did, too. How does my mother's murder fit into all this?"

"It doesn't," she looked shocked.

He couldn't help thinking about what Lorraine had said about his mother being too smart for her own good.

"I loved your mother," Norma said angrily. "I would have done anything for her."

"Even sleep with my father." He got up. "Why did you tell me my mother was having an affair?"

"I thought she was." Norma's gaze dropped. "Maybe I just wanted to believe it. It would have made things more...even."

"L.T. keeps an extra service revolver in the house," he said. "I need it and a box of cartridges."

Norma got to her feet, looking old and tired.

"We're going out to Evergreen," he said when she handed him the weapon and cartridges. "Carolyn Gray is still at large," he said, loading the weapon, then dumping a handful of extra cartridges into his coat pocket before slipping the gun in the other pocket. Without looking at Norma, he turned, taking Holly's hand, and headed for the door. "Give us twenty minutes to get out there, then call the chief. Tell him everything we've told you."

"Slade?"

He kept his back to her but stopped, knowing she wasn't going to ask him not to go to Evergreen. She knew him better than that. After all, she'd been like a mother to him.

"I'm sorry. But if I hadn't done what I did, you wouldn't be here."

"No," he said. "And, right now, that would be a blessing."

Holly didn't say a word as they climbed into the pickup and started toward Evergreen. She laid her hand on his thigh and seemed to watch the road ahead.

"Thanks," he said after a few miles, thankful that she hadn't asked a lot of questions or tried to offer him sympathy or even comfort right now.

"Rawlins, when this is all over I want us to take the baby to someplace warm," she said. "Have you ever been to Arizona?"

He glanced over at her, wondering if she felt as cold as he did inside. "No, but I'd go there with you."

She smiled. "Good." After a few minutes, she said, "Did I tell you I remembered the first time I met Dr. Allan Wellington? It was at a party right before Thanksgiving. I hate parties, but I went because Dr. Wellington supposedly wanted to buy some of my art. I had a splitting headache. He offered me a little something for it."

Slade glanced at her in the glow of the dash lights. She was staring out the window.

"Once he had control of my mind, he didn't need the pills anymore. I guess I should feel lucky that at least I wasn't taking the Halcion when I met you, when I got pregnant with our baby and during my pregnancy. Inez insisted I start taking the pills again right after I came home from the hospital because of the weird dreams I started having. Memories."

He drove for a few miles in the falling snow, silence between them.

"I guess he wanted a legitimate heir," Holly continued as if there hadn't been a break. "That's why he married me. I was lucky he died when he did. I guess he planned to impregnate me the way he had all his other 'mothers.'" She paused for a moment. "You thought I might have killed him for his *money*."

The pickup's lights cut through the snow and darkness. Ahead, Slade spotted the turnoff for Evergreen. He slowed the truck. He glanced over at her and frowned. "You think someone killed Dr. Wellington and made it look like a heart attack?"

"It's possible. Especially now that we know that Dr. Delaney was a friend of Allan's and part of all this."

"Sweet heaven." He couldn't help thinking of his father's heart attack.

He brought the pickup to a stop at the entrance to Evergreen Institute, the headlights shining through the snow to illuminate the gate. Only this time, he wasn't going to buzz in and let them know he was coming. He took the key ring Holly had found at Lorraine's and climbed out of the truck, leaving the pickup running, the headlights on, and, walked over to the lock.

It took him a few minutes. The snow fell around him silent as death. No wind up here. No sound but the hum of the pickup's engine behind him and the glow of the headlights.

He finally found the key that activated the gate. It swung open. Holly drove the pickup through, the gate closing soundlessly behind the truck.

She slid over as he got back in. He turned off the headlights and waited for his eyes to adjust. He could make out the pines along the edge of the road.

Slowly, he drove through the falling snow toward Evergreen. He'd noticed an employees' entrance road yesterday. It wound behind the Institute. Slade took it now. Through the snow, he saw a light glowing in the employees' parking lot. He followed it, stopping at the edge of the late afternoon darkness.

"We'll have to walk from here," he told Holly as he cut the engine. He wanted to tell her how he felt, all the emotions roiling inside him, one clear. He loved her. He loved their baby. "If something happens—"

She laughed softly. "What could *possibly* happen?" Then she touched his face, leaning toward him to kiss his lips. A soft, tender kiss.

Then he heard the click of her door opening as she slipped out. He followed her.

One of the keys on Lorraine's ring opened the employees' entrance. He'd half expected an alarm to go off. Or a dozen guys in white coats to appear the moment they stepped inside.

But no alarm sounded. No team of white coats. The door closed behind them. Slade stood with Holly in the silence, tense as a spring. Holly pointed down the dimly lit hallway, away from the section of Evergreen that resembled a country club to the part without the pool or tennis courts, without the spa and the gym. Toward the part that she said was closed to "clients."

The gun he'd taken from Norma's felt cold and heavy as a rock in his coat pocket. In his other pocket was the key ring and the extra cartridges.

He was counting on Dr. Allan Wellington's ego. The man couldn't have helped himself; he would have kept track of his babies just to feed that incredible ego. Slade was also counting on the person who'd taken over for Wellington to have the same type of egocentric character. So there would be a record of what had happened to their baby.

The problem was, Slade wasn't sure how much access Lorraine would have had. He didn't think she'd have had a key to the files. He'd probably have to break in. And Carolyn Gray was still at large. And, as far as Slade knew, armed and dangerous.

They reached a caged door with a sign announcing it Off Limits. Only authorized personnel. As quietly as he could, he tried one key, then another until almost the last one. The lock opened. Again, no alarm sounded. At least not one he and Holly could hear.

He glanced over at her. She looked scared but not about to stop now. That was his Holly.

They moved quickly, stepping through the door, closing it firmly behind them. This section looked like a hospital. Smelled like one, too. It was the smell that worried Slade. He pulled the weapon from his pocket and edged down the hallway. There were only four doors, the second one on the right standing open. He moved cautiously, motioning for Holly to stay behind him. The first two were examining rooms, the third, on the left, appeared to be an operating room.

He stopped just before the open doorway, took a breath, gripped the weapon in both hands, then started to step around it, ready to fire.

"Adding another breaking and entering charge to your record?" Chief L. T. Curtis asked as he stepped from what was obviously the lab. "I figured you'd show up here." He wagged his head at him. "Have you lost your mind, Slade?"

"Not yet. But the night is young." He assumed Curtis had spoken with Norma or he wouldn't already be here. Obviously Norma hadn't waited twenty minutes to call him.

"I thought you had more sense than to jeopardize your client's life as well as your own," the chief said.

"It's my baby who's missing," Holly snapped.

"I understand that," Curtis said, sounding almost compassionate, a stretch for him even on one of his good days. "But you have no business here. Neither of you do."

Slade looked past him. The lab had been vandalized, just as Delaney had told them. Slade felt his heart drop. "I think whoever took our baby kept records. I need to look in those files." He motioned to a huge set of file cabinets against the right-hand wall of the lab.

"You aren't searching anything," Curtis snapped. "I can have you both thrown in jail, and it appears that's what it's going to take."

"You should be out looking for Carolyn Gray, not busting my chops," Slade snapped back.

"We *are* looking for her. She was last seen inside the Institute. We've searched the entire place. We haven't found her, but that doesn't mean she isn't here. Now you listen to me," the chief continued. "I have a couple of police officers in the main office upstairs. I can either call them down here to remove you bodily. Or you can do this my way."

Slade glanced toward the file cabinets. They didn't look as if they'd been broken into. Yet. "You'd better go ahead and call your officers down here." He started to step past the cop.

The chief swore at he grabbed Slade's arm. "You want to add resisting arrest to all the other charges against you?"

They glared at each other for a long moment. Slade wondered if Norma had told the chief everything? It didn't seem the time to bring up her confession. Slade suspected her liaison with his father was one of the reasons the chief had never let himself get too close to

Slade and Shelley. Or maybe it was just the cop's nature.

Curtis let out a sigh. "Well, at least don't jeopardize Holly's life with your damned foolishness. Until Carolyn Gray is found, I want Holly with those two policemen upstairs—no argument," he snapped when Holly started to protest. "I'll take her up myself. When I get back down, I'll let you be present while I search the lab. That's the deal and believe me, it's a better deal than you deserve."

Slade saw his chance to be left alone here to search on his own. "He's right, Hol," he said quickly. "I'll feel much better knowing you're safe." Hurriedly, he pulled her to him and whispered, "I have a better chance of finding something without the chief here."

She kissed him and nodded, obviously not liking it but realizing if she didn't go along with it, the cop would force them both to go with him. "Be careful."

"Always."

"Come on," the chief said. "Wait right here," he ordered Slade. "You touch anything and it will be inadmissible as evidence."

He was no longer looking for evidence. He just wanted his baby. "Got it."

Curtis shot him a look. "I mean it, Slade. I'll put your ass behind bars so fast your head will swim."

Slade waited until Curtis and Holly disappeared through the locked doors and around the corner before he hurried into the lab.

The room was large with ceiling-high cabinets along the left wall, what looked like a huge walk-in cooler at the rear and a lab setup and office off to the right. Someone had broken a lot of the glassware and smashed some of the equipment. Strange, it looked more like vandalism than anything else. Certainly not the kind of thing he thought Carolyn Gray would do to cover her trail.

Slade moved to the desk and quickly checked the drawers. Nothing of interest. But on the wall over the desk was a plaque that read:

The question of genetic quality of the coming generations is a hundred times more important than the conflict between capitalism and socialism and a thousand times more important than the struggle between Germany and other countries.

Fritz Lenz, leading German eugenicist.

Next to it was another:

Eugenics: the movement devoted to improving the human species through the control of hereditary factors in mating.

Sweet heaven.

He turned to the row of steel file cabinets. This time, he doubted he'd find a key on Lorraine's ring. He was right. No key.

He glanced around for something to try to pry open the cabinets with. He found a metal letter opener in the top desk drawer, broke each of the locks and drew out one drawer after another.

They were all empty.

Whoever had cleaned them out had a key. So why bother to make it look like the place had been vandalized? Unless whoever had done it was in a hurry and didn't have the time or patience to break the locks on the files.

Had Carolyn had the key all along? Slade doubted it. She must have taken it from Dr. Delaney. No wonder they hadn't been able to find the keys to his Suburban.

He glanced over at the cabinets lining the wall across the room, doubting Carolyn had left anything. She'd known exactly what she was looking for, it seemed.

And yet, his only hope was that she might have missed something. He started toward the cabinets, slowing as he spotted something dark pooling beneath one of the far cabinets.

He pulled the weapon from his pocket and moved cautiously toward the cabinet.

HOLLY BARELY HEARD what Chief L. T. Curtis said as she walked beside him down the hall. All she could think about was Slade back there alone in the lab. She hadn't wanted to leave him, but she knew that if she hadn't, Curtis would have forced them both to go. Selfishly, all she could hope was that Slade would find what they needed. A lead to their daughter.

Let Curtis bring down Carolyn Gray and see that she got her proper punishment. Holly just wanted her daughter—and Slade.

The chief was talking about Slade, how stubborn he'd always been, telling stories about Slade as a teenager. "He's been obsessed with his mother's murder for as long as I can remember."

So the cop didn't know that Norma had told Slade the truth. "That seems pretty normal," she said, only half listening. This part of the Institute seemed completely abandoned. She could hear nothing but the sound of their footsteps and the cop's voice. Her mind, however, was on Slade and what he would find. He had to find *something*.

"Shelley doesn't just look like her brother," Curtis was saying. "Smart as a whip, that one. Always had to be careful around her. She never missed a trick."

"I'm sure you and Norma love them like your own children," she said. Somewhere deep in the bowels of this place she could hear what sounded like water running. Or maybe it was the heating system cranking out warm air, trying to heat this monstrosity. "I'm a little confused about where we are." They'd been walking, it seemed, for some time and yet she hadn't seen the entrance she and Slade had come in. Nor any elevator or stairs.

"This place is much larger than you would think from looking at it on the outside," he said. "The guy who had this place built thought the world was going to come to an end, so he had this part put in separately from the main house. The walls are made of reinforced concrete four feet thick. You could drop a bomb on this place and it would stay standing." He seemed to realize she wasn't listening. "So fill me in on what you know about this baby thing."

"I'm sure Norma told you most of it."

"Norma was too upset, she wasn't making much sense."

Holly told him about the three monsters huddled at the end of her bed during her delivery in the abandoned part of the hospital.

"So you think they were Dr. Delaney, Lorraine Vogel and this nurse, Carolyn Gray?" he said.

"Yes, except…"

"What's wrong?" he asked.

She frowned as she remembered something. "I have

this memory of one of them talking to me and this distinct feeling that I knew the person. I remember being shocked because it was the last person I would have suspected. But I didn't know Lorraine or Dr. Delaney or Carolyn Gray.''

''That is odd. Maybe you'd just heard one of them somewhere and thought you recognized the voice,'' he suggested.

Out of the corner of her eye, she saw him clutch his side. ''Are you all right?''

''Just a little indigestion. Slade gives it to me all the time.''

She spotted both stairs and elevator down the hall. She was anxious to get off this level. The echo of their steps along the concrete hallway was giving her a headache. The halls seemed to wind like a maze down here. She felt turned around, but then she hadn't been paying attention.

Unconsciously, now that she could see the elevator ahead, she slowed her steps, trying to give Slade as much time alone as possible in the lab.

''I wouldn't worry if I were you,'' the chief was saying. ''We have a warrant out on Carolyn Gray, the crime lab is sending someone down from Missoula to help us with the investigation of Dr. Delaney's murder, and we'll continue to look for your baby.'' He ran his beefy hand over his face. ''One way or the other, it will be over soon,'' he said, his hand muffling his voice. ''So don't you worry.''

They had almost reached the end of the hallway and the elevator. Her heart slammed against her chest. She stumbled, losing her balance.

Curtis grabbed her to steady her. ''Are you all right?''

This time she saw him flinch. Something was definitely wrong with him, but her mind was on the flash of memory. It moved through her mind like a wisp of cloud. She could feel him staring at her oddly. Just get to the elevator, she told herself. "I think I'd like to sit down once we get to the main office."

"No problem," the chief said as he took her arm. "Let's get you taken care of as quickly as possible so I can get back to your...boyfriend."

SLADE COULD SMELL the blood pooling in front of the cabinet as he drew near. He reached out cautiously for the knob, half expecting the cabinet door to be locked. He pulled. The door swung open.

Carolyn Gray tumbled out.

One good look at her, and Slade knew there was no reason to check for a pulse. She'd been shot and shoved into the cabinet as if her killer had been in a hurry. He could see now where the blood that had splattered on the white tile floor had been hastily wiped up.

He stumbled back, confused. Three monsters. All dead. If Carolyn had killed Dr. Delaney, then who had killed her? Not Lorraine. Carolyn's body was still warm and Lorraine—

He jumped at the sudden sound of his cell phone ringing. Hurriedly, he dug the phone out of his shirt pocket before it could ring again. "Rawlins." He'd expected it to be Holly warning him that the cop was on his way back down.

"Slade?" It was Shelley. "Is everything all right?"

Not a chance. "Yeah."

"I got your message. Sorry I didn't get back to you sooner. I was farther up island."

He started to cut her off, to tell her this really wasn't

a good time, but then she said, "You asked about the Christmas ornament. The twin golden angels?"

He'd almost forgotten, so much had been going on. He moved away from Carolyn's body, toward the door.

"I *do* remember it," Shelley was saying. "You know who made it? Francie Dunn. You know, Jerry Dunn's mom. That was back when we were kids and played together."

He'd forgotten that Jerry had lived down the street from them back then. When he'd called Shelley, he'd hoped maybe the ornament had meant something to their mother—their adoptive mother, he mentally corrected himself.

"So Francie Dunn gave it to Mom," he said.

"No, Francie *made* it. L.T. gave it to Mom that Christmas, right before…"

He stopped in mid-step, freezing. That Christmas, right before she was murdered? "You're sure L.T. gave it to her?"

"Positive. I remember because she looked at him and burst into tears. That was so unlike Mom. Slade, what's going on? Why ask about the ornament now?"

He was trying to understand his mother's reaction and why the chief would have given her the twin angels. Norma said he'd been against the pregnancy. He'd never been close to either Slade or Shelley—and he definitely wasn't an angel kind of guy. Unless there was some special meaning other than the fact that the angels were twins that had made his mother cry.

"Slade, what's going on?" Shelley asked, sounding worried. "Has something happened?"

"You know me, I just get sentimental this time of year."

"Oh yeah, right. You're sure everything is all right?"

"It's fine. Shel, I've got to go. I love you." He snapped off the phone before she could question him further and turned to find Chief L. T. Curtis framed in the lab doorway.

Chapter Seventeen

Holly woke in total blackness, dazed, head aching. The last thing she remembered was reaching for the elevator button.

She tried to get up and bumped into a wall in the dark. She could hear the sound of water and heat pipes but couldn't tell if they were over her head—or just one misstep below her. Carefully, she got to her feet, afraid of falling into an abyss.

Once on her feet, she discovered the knot on the side of her head. She half expected to find no memory of anything. But not only could she remember being hit, she remembered the voice and the muffled familiar words. "It will be over soon." The same words she'd heard the night she delivered her baby. And she realized now why she'd known the person speaking the words even through his mask. Why she'd been so shocked. Because she'd met Chief L. T. Curtis last February with Slade, right before someone had wiped Slade from her mind—but not from her heart, she thought.

No wonder the monsters had found her soon after she met Chief Curtis.

But at least now she knew she'd gone to Slade this

Christmas Eve of her own free will, because she was
in trouble and instinctively she'd known to go to him.

And now she had her memory back, for all the good
it did her. Slade was waiting at the lab. And Curtis had
told him he'd be back as soon as he took care of Holly.
Well, he'd taken care of her all right!

Gingerly, she reached out her arms, fearing what she
might feel in the dark, but desperately needing to escape this prison—and get to Slade. He would trust
Chief Curtis. He would believe that she was safe with
the two police officers she'd bet weren't waiting upstairs in the main office. Slade would be a sitting duck.

Her fingertips touched a wall directly in front of her.
And another off to her left and right. A closet? Or a
coffin stood on end? The thought sent a chill through
her. She felt for a doorknob, desperate to find one.

Her hand found the handle of a broom or mop and
shoved it aside, only to have it hit something over her
head. A large container tumbled down, striking her
shoulder, almost knocking her to her knees.

She grabbed her shoulder in the blackness of the
closet and felt something wet and sticky. Blood? She
leaned against the wall, holding her shoulder, waiting
for the pain to subside a little. The closet smelled
strongly of floor cleaner. She crouched down and found
a large plastic bottle and something wet and sticky
spilled on the floor. Not blood. Floor cleaner.

She wasn't bleeding. That was a relief anyway.

She wiped her hands on her jeans and went back to
looking for a doorknob. Nor was she in a coffin, she
thought counting her meager blessings.

Her hand banged against metal. Smooth, round
metal. She'd never been so happy to find a doorknob
in her life. She tried to turn it, not terribly surprised to

find the door locked—and obviously with a key—from the outside.

She considered throwing herself against the door, but knew that breaking it down was out of the question even if she'd had enough room to get a run at it. Banging on the door for help seemed just as ridiculous. She hadn't seen a soul on her walk with the chief down the labyrinth of hallways. Wherever she was, it wasn't on a main floor and she would never be heard over the sound of the water and heating system now roaring in her ears.

She was trapped. In the dark. And Slade was out there with at least two crazy armed people—Carolyn Gray and Chief L. T. Curtis.

She fought the desire to scream. Or cry. *Think.* She felt around for the broom or mop handle she'd discovered earlier. Mop, she decided, when she found it and ran her fingers the length of it.

Maybe she could use it as leverage to break off the doorknob. She wasn't sure the door would open even if she managed such a feat, but she had to try. She couldn't just stand here in the broom closet, unable to warn Slade, just waiting for the chief of police or Carolyn Gray to come back and kill her.

She got the mop handle between the wall and the knob and pulled down with all her strength. She thought she felt it give a little. If only she had a little more room. Or more weight. The mop handle broke. She fell, slamming into the closet wall.

She felt tears rush her eyes and a sob catch in her throat, just waiting to be let loose. She threw down the piece of broken mop handle, hurt and scared and frustrated. And angry. But she wasn't going to cry.

Bracing herself against the wall, she put her foot

against the doorknob. She would break the thing even if it killed her!

She kicked, then kicked harder, ignoring the pain in her arch. The doorknob gave way on the ninth kick. It clattered to the floor. She leaned against the wall, realizing she was crying, but not sure how long she had been.

She wiped the tears from her face with her sleeve and turned her back to the wall opposite the door, figuring she'd have to kick her way out, but determined she would, come hell or high water.

The moment her boot touched the door, the door swung open and she slipped on the floor cleaner and fell to the floor. Crying and laughing and closet-blind, she scrambled to her feet and burst out into the dim light of the hallway.

Once out, she realized she had no idea how to get back to the lab.

SLADE HADN'T HEARD the chief open the door because he'd been on the phone. Curtis stood filling the doorway, his service revolver in his beefy hand. He was looking at Carolyn Gray's body, his expression one of regret rather than surprise.

"Who was on the phone?" the cop asked.

"Wrong number."

"You always were a bad liar, Slade. I figured Shelley would remember the ornament incident. She always paid more attention to the little things than you did."

Slade stared at him, trying to get control of his fury, his fear, his repulsion, trying to understand with his mind something his heart just refused to believe. "What did you do with Holly?" he demanded, fear making his blood run cold as he advanced on the cop.

Curtis lifted the revolver in his hand, the threat too clear.

Slade stopped, his own weapon in his coat pocket, where he'd put it when he'd found Carolyn dead. He knew he couldn't get it out, aim and pull the trigger before Curtis fired and killed him, so he didn't even consider it. He wouldn't do Holly any good dead.

"I locked her in a closet until we could get some things sorted out," the cop said.

He didn't know why, but he believed Curtis. "Why?" he asked, his heart breaking. "Why would you get involved with someone like Allan Wellington?"

"Allan was a genius," Curtis said.

"All madmen think they're geniuses."

"Do they? You think I'm mad and yet I'm no genius. If I were I wouldn't be here right now." The cop glanced toward Carolyn Gray's body. "I wish you'd left this alone, Slade. I told you Marcella would never have had an affair."

Slade eyed the contents of the lab, looking for something he could use for a weapon. A small microscope lay on its side on the lab table in a pile of broken glass. If he could get to it—

"Marcella must have found out what Wellington was doing when she was getting the fertility treatments," Slade said, edging slowly toward the lab table. "She would have come to you, because for some reason she didn't want my father to know she was getting treatments? Or trying to expose Dr. Wellington." He frowned as he glanced at Curtis. "And she would have trusted you." A thought struck him. "She found out about your involvement."

The cop was nodding thoughtfully. "I didn't want to hurt Marcella, but she wouldn't listen to reason."

Slade swore. "She was trying to tell us who her murderer was. You gave her that ornament as a warning. If she talked you'd do something to her kids. No, not her kids, Norma's and Joe's kids."

"So Norma told you," Curtis said disgustedly. "I figured eventually she would." His gaze hardened. "They betrayed me. Especially Marcella. She's the one who talked Norma into having Joe's children, and Norma—" he shook his head angrily "—jumped at the chance to be with your father."

"That's why you stole Holly's and my baby," Slade said with a start. "You couldn't stand the thought of Norma having a grandchild."

"You always were a bright kid," the cop said. "Must have gotten that from your father."

His father. Slade looked into Curtis's eyes and knew. "You made it look like a heart attack." *He never had a bad heart.* Inez's words seem to echo. Sweet heaven. "You killed my father—and Dr. Wellington." It was everything he could do not to launch himself at the man and take his chances. If he could just get his hands around the cop's throat— "Dad must have found out that you were the one who killed Marcella."

"Your father was one hell of a cop," Curtis said almost sadly. "He wanted to blow me away himself, but he had too much honor. It was just one of the things Norma loved about him. He gave me until the next morning to turn myself in. Wellington told me what I needed to make the death look like a heart attack. Ironically, I used the same drug on the good doctor when the time came."

"But why kill Wellington if he was such a genuis?"

Slade asked, trying to put it all together, knowing somewhere in it all was the key to what had happened to his baby girl.

"He was getting out of control and I was getting tired of cleaning up after him. And I didn't need him anymore."

"Holly," Slade guessed, inching toward the lab table. He moved so slowly. Too slowly. But he didn't dare make a misstep. He had to think of Holly. Finding Holly. "You were afraid of him marrying a woman so much younger and controlling her mind through the use of drugs."

"Wellington had taken her off the drug so he could get her pregnant, but he was having trouble controlling her."

"It was you she was running from when she left the Institute last Christmas Eve," Slade said. It all made sense now. The way Holly had disappeared right after she'd met the chief and Norma. "You could have killed her after you used the mind control to make her forget me," he said, wondering if there wasn't some human compassion in the man.

"You were already obsessed over your mother's murder," Curtis snapped. "If I'd killed Holly, you would never have let up until you found out the truth."

Slade was almost within reach of the table—and the microscope. Suddenly he saw something that stopped him dead. He watched a drop of blood fall from the cop's left side and splat on the floor, bright red, at the man's feet. Slade's glaze leapt to Curtis' zipped jacket. The knit band around the bottom on the left was soaked with blood. He'd been wounded! Had Carolyn Gray fought back? But how badly was the cop hurt? "You had to know she was carrying my baby, Norma's grandbaby.''

"Inez convinced me that the baby was Wellington's."

Slade saw it now, all of the pieces finally falling into place. Except one large empty hole that he had to have filled no matter what happened in this room tonight.

HOLLY STOOD in the middle of the hallway, lost. She had no idea where she was or where the lab was. She felt tears blur her vision. She swiped at them angrily. Which way? Back down the hall away from the elevator? But then the halls made a junction and—

She saw something on the floor and knew before she reached down to touch the bright red spot what had been wrong with Chief Curtis. Blood. He'd been wounded. It made no sense, but she didn't question it as she looked down the hallway for another drop of blood, then another. Better than a breadcrumb trail, she thought.

She took off her boots, not wanting to make a sound, then began to follow the bloody trail back to the lab. As she drew closer, she began to run, fear and anger coursing through her veins like blood, a hot cauldron of fury. "Dammit, Rawlins, don't you dare let that psychopath kill you!"

"WHAT IS IT you want, Slade?" The way Curtis said it he could have been asking him what he wanted for lunch. The cop sounded tired and old and Slade found himself wondering how well he'd ever known him.

"My baby and Holly."

Curtis cocked his head to the side. "Why don't I believe that's all you want?"

"That's it. I don't give a damn about the rest of this." It surprised him, but it was true.

The cop grabbed a shelf on the wall next to him and flung its contents to the floor. "Not you, Slade. You have to have truth *and* justice. You couldn't live with yourself otherwise."

"You might be surprised," Slade said.

Curtis wagged his bald head as he pulled a second gun from his coat.

Slade recognized it as his own—the one he couldn't find at Dr. Delaney's. "Dr. Delaney was telling the truth. He wasn't at the birth of Holly's and my baby. It was you. You put the mask in Delaney's closet to frame him." He could reach the microscope now. All he needed was the right moment and a hell of a lot of luck. "There is one thing I don't understand. Why not let Holly keep the baby? All Inez wanted was an heir for her brother—even a dead one. Why not let Inez have a live family heir? No one would be the wiser."

"Holly was too unstable," Curtis said with a sigh. "I figured after her baby was born dead, she'd probably end up committing suicide."

He'd planned to kill Holly. No doubt still did. Sweet heaven. "What part did Dr. Delaney and Dr. O'Brien play in all this?"

The question seemed to take Curtis by surprise. He frowned. "Dr. O'Brien has nothing to do with this. Why would you ask about him?"

Slade spotted Holly out of the corner of his eye and couldn't believe it for a moment. She peeked around the edge of the doorframe and winked at him. He'd never been so glad to see anyone in his life.

"I saw O'Brien at Inez's," Slade said.

The cop's frown deepened. "Inez and Dr. O'Brien?

She told me she was just trying to get Holly recommitted, and Dr. O'Brien had offered to help."

It was obvious Curtis wasn't so sure about Inez now. "You know there is something that bothers me," Slade said, motioning to the lab, actually motioning to the microscope on the lab table, hoping that Holly would see what he had planned. "You don't give a damn about superbabies or changing the world to meet some master plan. What were you really doing here?"

Holly nodded. She had her boots off. One in each hand. She motioned that she could throw them.

"Haven't you already guessed? At first, I was just angry that Norma and I couldn't have children when all the wrong couples were having babies. Then I realized there was money to be made with the babies that didn't quite stack up. Allan thought I...disposed of them. But babies, I found, are worth much more alive, either in hard cash or to pay off a debt."

Slade wanted to kill the man with his bare hands, but instead he nodded at Holly as if answering Curtis. "Was my baby cash or payment of a debt?"

"A debt. I was shutting down. Wellington had needed someone to clean up his messes, so we had a pretty good thing going until he became too much of a liability. Your baby was going to be my last...deal. Had a good run, no reason to push my luck."

"But then Holly began to remember," Slade said.

The cop nodded. "Having your baby be stillborn, it's really made you crazy. And when it all comes out about Dr. Wellington and his mind control...well, everyone involved will be dead. I think I'll retire, too broken up about your death to continue law enforcement. Holly will commit suicide. That shouldn't surprise anyone. Once I get her back under my control again. My old method doesn't work, thanks to Dr. Delaney. I knew the day would come when his conscience would get to him. But he's gone now. All I have to worry about is Shelley. I'm sorry, Slade, but I think all of Norma's children and grandchildren are going to have to die.''

A thought lodged itself in Slade's brain like a splinter. The three monsters in Holly's painting. He'd thought they were Carolyn Gray, Lorraine Vogel and Dr. Delaney. Why hadn't he remembered that the monsters didn't seem to know what they were doing? Delaney had delivered thousands of babies. He wouldn't have panicked. But Delaney hadn't been there—Curtis had.

"What went wrong during Holly's delivery?" he asked the cop, positioning himself to grab the microscope the moment Holly threw the boots.

"Nothing," Curtis said, momentarily distracted by the question. "Just a little surprise. We were expecting one baby—not two!''

"Twins?" Slade shot a look to Holly. Curtis caught the look and started to turn. "Now!" Slade yelled.

Holly threw the boots and ducked back out of the doorway. Slade grabbed the microscope and lunged at the cop.

But Curtis was in good shape and quick for a man of his age. He swung back around, realizing Slade was the greatest threat. The microscope hit the cop's hand, the gun went clattering across the floor, and then Curtis was on him, the second gun, Slade's own, in the big man's hand.

They fell to the floor, wrestling for the weapon.

"Get the other gun!" Slade cried to Holly as he and

Curtis fought, Slade's pistol between them, Curtis strong as a bull.

She ran into the lab. Curtis's service revolver had slid under one of the cabinets near Carolyn's body. Slade saw Holly cringe at the sight of the dead woman, then flatten herself to the floor to reach back under the cabinet. Everything was happening so fast, and yet it seemed in slow motion, each detail so clear. He could see that she'd cut her bare foot on some glass, blood soaking through her sock, but she seemed oblivious of the wound as she dug for the weapon, unable to reach it.

Slade struggled for the gun between them, Curtis rolling so he was on top.

The blast surprised Slade when the gun went off.

For a moment he didn't know which of them had been hit. Maybe neither. Then he felt something wet and hot across his chest. Curtis was still fighting for the gun, not appearing harmed in anyway.

Slade didn't think he'd been hit, but he knew gunshot victims often went into shock, unaware for a few minutes that they'd been injured. He got an elbow up to Curtis's throat and with effort shoved the man off him. Curtis tumbled backwards, coming down hard, but the cop still had Slade's gun in his hand.

"I've got it!" Slade heard Holly yell. She sent the cop's revolver skidding across the floor to Slade. Out of the corner of his eye, he saw Curtis swing his arm up to fire, the barrel of the gun pointed at Holly.

Slade grabbed the skidding revolver, knowing he wasn't going to make it in time.

Another gunshot echoed through the lab. Slade had the revolver and was bringing it up to fire at Curtis, but he didn't get a shot off. He heard Holly gasp, heard someone enter the lab. He swung the barrel of the gun toward the door as Dr. O'Brien filled the doorway, a gun in his hand.

"FBI, drop your weapon!" O'Brien yelled, just before Slade could squeeze off a shot.

"FBI?" Slade dropped his gun.

Holly was screaming at O'Brien. "You killed him! You killed him before he told us where our babies are!"

Slade took her in his arms. "It's okay, Hol, I think I know where our babies are," he whispered. He looked over her shoulder at O'Brien. FBI? "Where the hell have you been?"

"Right behind you, following the trail of death and destruction you left in your wake," the FBI agent snapped. He turned to Holly. "I tried to get you into protective custody by having you re-admit yourself to Evergreen, then I could have protected you."

"Could you have?" she challenged. "Then you knew it was Chief Curtis?"

"No," O'Brien admitted. "That I didn't know. But I've been working this case undercover since Dr. Parris called me in on it. He'd discovered the Genesis Project and contacted my office."

"It would have helped if you'd told us who you were," Slade said as he helped Holly to her feet, keeping his arm around her, never planning to let her go ever again.

"I couldn't be sure just what your involvement was," O'Brien said. "From the information I was getting from Inez Wellington... That day I passed you on the road to her place, I'd just found out that she'd been leading me on a wild goose chase." He shook his head.

"Where do you think you're going?" he said as Slade and Holly moved toward the door.

"To see my pharmacist," Slade said.

"Jerry Dunn?" O'Brien asked. "We have a warrant for his arrest on interstate trafficking of drugs."

"Add kidnapping to the charge," Slade said. "We're going to go get our babies. I hope you aren't going to try to stop us."

The FBI agent backed off. "I'll need statements from both of you later."

Slade nodded, then he and Holly headed for town.

"Rawlins, how can you be so sure Jerry Dunn has our babies?" Holly asked as they neared town.

"Curtis said he used them to pay a debt. It dawned on me. Who else had to be involved? Someone who could supply the drugs. Patty Dunn was one of the names I saw on the list of Genesis Project patients. Jerry's father was also a pharmacist. He did so well in a little town like Dry Creek that he retired and gave Jerry the drugstore."

"You think Jerry's father was involved with Allan?"

"Yeah." Delaney had said this had been going on for more than thirty years. It just finally made sense.

JERRY DUNN answered the door. Behind him, Slade could hear the sound of babies crying. He pushed his way in. "Chief Curtis is dead. The FBI are on their way."

Patty Dunn sat on the couch, rocking the two infants in the double baby carrier. "If one cries, the other one does," she said and looked up, obviously surprised to see Slade and Holly.

"That's how my sister and I were," Slade said as

he moved to the carrier and looked down at the identical twins. They had the Rawlins' dimples and Holly's blue eyes.

"Oh God," Holly said and dropped to her knees beside the babies.

Patty Dunn looked from her babies to her husband. "Jerry?" Jerry said nothing. Behind him, FBI agent O'Brien appeared in the doorway with several police officers.

Slade picked up one of the babies and handed her to Holly. Holly began to cry as she held her baby for the first time. He picked up the other infant and cradled her in his arms. The one Holly held stopped crying, and a moment later the one in Slade's arms did as well. He smiled down at the infant in his arms and couldn't hold back his own tears.

Behind him he could hear Jerry being arrested and read his rights along with his wife, Patty. A female officer said Patty's other two children, the two boys Slade had seen in the photograph at the pharmacy, would be taken into police custody.

Slade looked over at Holly. "I was just thinking. You know what you said about going someplace warm? I think we should head south. Someplace tropical, maybe. Someplace we could get married."

She had been gazing in awe back and forth at the two identical baby girls they held. Now she looked up with a start. "Rawlins, are you asking me to marry you?"

"What do you think?" he asked, his heart in his throat.

"I think it's about time!"

Epilogue

The following Christmas Eve

Holly sat on the couch smiling. Christmas music played on the stereo while Slade and Shelley and her new husband, John, helped the twins decorate the tree.

"How are you feeling?" Norma asked as she came into the room and handed Holly a cup of hot cocoa.

"Better."

Norma sat down beside her. "I never thought I'd see this day."

Holly reached over to take her hand and gave it a squeeze. The last year seemed like a blur now. She and Slade and the twins had flown to Tobago to join Shelley. They'd gotten married there, on a white sand beach, the sound of the turquoise surf in the background and the twins watching from the shade of the cabana.

Back home, Jerry Dunn had told the FBI everything he knew, including how his father had worked with Dr. Allan Wellington and how he'd taken his father's place. Jerry had been the bell-ringer outside on Christmas Eve. He'd called Carolyn Gray to warn her at that point. Curtis hadn't known yet. Inez was arrested in the hospital, but didn't live long enough to see jail. She took an overdose of Halcion. Jerry's wife, Patty, cleared of charges, filed for divorce, took her sons and left town.

It had taken the FBI a while to sort everything out. But following in the footsteps of egomaniac Dr. Allan Wellington, L. T. Curtis had kept a record not only of the births he'd "manipulated" but the lives he'd taken, starting with Roy Vogel's twenty years ago. Dr. Wellington hadn't been happy with his first son's development and decided it was time to terminate that "experiment" and provide a killer for Marcella Rawlins murder.

From there, Curtis had killed as needed, always able to cover it easily as police chief. His next victim had been Joe Rawlins when Joe discovered the truth about Marcella's death.

Along with the cop's records of events were Wellington's accounts of using mind control on Holly. It seemed the doctor had been taken with her and decided he should have a child with her, but was killed by Curtis before he could artificially inseminate Holly. Wellington had always been incapable of conceiving in any other way but through artificial insemination.

Unfortunately for Curtis, Holly had seen him inject Dr. Wellington with the drug that caused his heart attack. The cop tried to control Holly through mind control and drugs with Inez's help but he feared it was just a matter of time before Holly remembered Wellington's death and told Inez. Curtis had tried to kill her the Christmas Eve she ran away from Evergreen Institute and into Slade's headlights.

For two months, the cop had searched for her. Then to his delight, she'd turned up with Slade. The cop reprogrammed her that evening on the phone and had her steal some files—including the one on Slade's mother—and some money, hoping that would be the end of it.

But of course it wasn't.

It all made sense now. Why Holly hadn't wanted Slade to go to the police when he'd found her in the snowstorm. Why she'd been afraid for her life.

After a few weeks in Tobago, waiting for everything to die down, Slade and Holly and the twins returned home to Montana.

"You know we don't have to stay in Dry Creek," Slade had said.

"No, Rawlins, we don't. But we will," she said smiling as she'd leaned over to kiss him. "Because it's home."

His eyes had widened. "We're going to have to buy a house!"

She'd laughed. "One with an art studio and a big backyard."

They'd found a house—right next door to Shelley's and closed on it the same day Shelley announced her engagement to John, the wonderful man she'd met while vacationing in Tobago.

It had taken time for Slade to forgive Norma. Then, one day when Norma had stopped over, Holly heard him tell the twins, "This is your gramma." Holly felt tears come to her eyes even now, just remembering the look on Norma's face.

Norma had been a part of their family ever since. The family was growing too; Shelley and John were expecting in March.

"You've been through a lot," Holly said now to

Norma as the Christmas tree started taking shape to the sound of "Jingle Bells" and laughter.

"Pish," Norma said. "I've been through nothing compared to you and Slade and the twins. No, I mean Slade. I never thought I'd see the day that he would actually be enjoying Christmas again."

Holly tried not to cry. She was so emotional these days. Just the sight of Slade and the twins made her close to tears of happiness. "I can't tell you how thankful I am to have him and our little angels."

"You don't have to," Norma said. "Believe me, I know."

Courtney toddled over with one of the ornaments cradled in her small hands. "Oook," she said smiling up at her grandmother.

Carmen toddled over to take a look at her twin's ornament, then showed her grandmother hers. "Look, angels, Gramma."

"They're beautiful," Norma said of the ornaments. "Just like the two of you!"

"Are you ready?" Shelley called out. She nodded to John to do the honors. He plugged in the lights.

The tree lit up, a warm glow of bright colored ornaments and twinkling lights.

"It's beautiful," Holly breathed, unable this time to hold back the tears. The twins climbed up onto the couch, one on each side of her, their eyes huge with surprise and excitement.

Slade sat down on the floor at her feet. "How are you feeling?" he asked, putting his hand on Holly's swollen belly. He smiled up at her as he felt a small foot kick.

"Rawlins, what would you think about having

Christmas babies?'' she asked as she felt another contraction coming.

"Are you serious?'' he cried getting onto his knees in front of her. "You don't mean...*now?*''

In an instant, he was on his feet. "She's going to have the babies!''

Shelley was at his side. "Take it easy. Go get her suitcase and start the pickup. Mom and I and Johnny can take care of Courtney and Carmen. But who's going to take care of Slade?''

Slade hadn't moved. He was looking down at Holly, his eyes so filled with love Holly thought she would burst.

"I just want this time to be...different,'' he said quietly.

"It will be, Rawlins,'' she said, smiling up at him. "This time I'm having twin boys!''

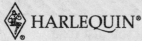

If you enjoyed what you just read,
then we've got an offer you can't resist!

Take 2 bestselling
love stories FREE!
Plus get a FREE surprise gift!

Clip this page and mail it to Harlequin Reader Service®

IN U.S.A.
3010 Walden Ave.
P.O. Box 1867
Buffalo, N.Y. 14240-1867

IN CANADA
P.O. Box 609
Fort Erie, Ontario
L2A 5X3

YES! Please send me 2 free Harlequin Intrigue® novels and my free surprise gift. After receiving them, if I don't wish to receive anymore, I can return the shipping statement marked cancel. If I don't cancel, I will receive 4 brand-new novels each month, before they're available in stores! In the U.S.A., bill me at the bargain price of $3.80 plus 25¢ shipping and handling per book and applicable sales tax, if any*. In Canada, bill me at the bargain price of $4.21 plus 25¢ shipping and handling per book and applicable taxes**. That's the complete price and a savings of at least 10% off the cover prices—what a great deal! I understand that accepting the 2 free books and gift places me under no obligation ever to buy any books. I can always return a shipment and cancel at any time. Even if I never buy another book from Harlequin, the 2 free books and gift are mine to keep forever.

181 HEN DC7U
381 HEN DC7V

Name	(PLEASE PRINT)
Address	Apt.#
City	State/Prov.	Zip/Postal Code

* Terms and prices subject to change without notice. Sales tax applicable in N.Y.
** Canadian residents will be charged applicable provincial taxes and GST.
  All orders subject to approval. Offer limited to one per household and not valid to current Harlequin Intrigue® subscribers.
  ® are registered trademarks of Harlequin Enterprises Limited.

INT01

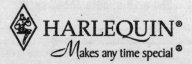

CALL THE ONES YOU LOVE OVER THE HOLIDAYS!

Save $25 off future book purchases when you buy any four Harlequin® or Silhouette® books in October, November and December 2001,

PLUS

receive a phone card good for 15 minutes of long-distance calls to anyone you want in North America!

WHAT AN INCREDIBLE DEAL!

Just fill out this form and attach 4 proofs of purchase (cash register receipts) from October, November and December 2001 books, and Harlequin Books will send you a coupon booklet worth a total savings of $25 off future purchases of Harlequin® and Silhouette® books, AND a 15-minute phone card to call the ones you love, anywhere in North America.

Please send this form, along with your cash register receipts as proofs of purchase, to:
In the USA: Harlequin Books, P.O. Box 9057, Buffalo, NY 14269-9057
In Canada: Harlequin Books, P.O. Box 622, Fort Erie, Ontario L2A 5X3
Cash register receipts must be dated no later than December 31, 2001.
Limit of 1 coupon booklet and phone card per household.
Please allow 4-6 weeks for delivery.

I accept your offer! Enclosed are 4 proofs of purchase.
Please send me my coupon booklet
and a 15-minute phone card:

Name: _____

Address: _____ City: _____

State/Prov.: _____ Zip/Postal Code: _____

Account Number (if available): _____

---

097 KJB DAGL
PHQ4013